DEATH OF A
DARK SOUL

BOOK 8 IN A FAIRY TALE SERIES

Find us Instagram and Tik Tok @afairytaleseries

Dedication:
This book is dedicated to Marsha

Reynolds, a wonderful woman who
loves my stories more then I do!

THE DARK FAE

The first fae brought with her the power of the silver light and the dark energy. Sisue herself was bathed in the golden light of the life force. When she gave the power to the women of fae, it was the ethereal string that she gave to them all. As their powers were sung in one by one, the silver light grew stronger. The dark energy began to grow jealous.

The dark energy has always been more powerful, because there is power in destruction. Long ago the dark energy and the silver light had split from the life force. One brings life and one brings death, because everything must exist in pairs.

The dark energy would whisper in the ears of the young fae. It promised power and strength. It promised freedom from the fae way of life. The heart of a fae is a powerful thing though, made by the golden light. Few would listen to the dark whispers.

The few who did, became mad from the darkness that engulfed them. The dark energy cannot be harnessed like the silver light, instead it must be set free. Very few of those who embraced the dark energy survived for long. Those who did though, became powerful creatures to behold.

During the Great War, only the dark fae fought back against the enemy sent to kill them all. Five planets attacked and the dark fae fought them fearlessly. They would unleash the madness hidden in the soldiers' minds, upon them. Only the dark fae, can truly see what lies in a man's heart. Now only one among them lives. The most powerful dark fae to ever be born. She has embraced the darkness and it serves her now. Her soul is as black as a starless night, yet her heart remains that of a fae.

She has never met an enemy she couldn't defeat, but she has never met a human.

CHAPTER 1

Amme sat on her throne, looking down at the crowd gathered below. For ten thousand years she had reigned over the people of Thelry. In fact, she has reigned over the galaxy. When she destroyed the Emperor and his planet, she had taken control. She watched as bloodlines of kings and queens died out and new ones sprung up to replace them. She had watched as technology became more advanced. She had seen fashion trends come and go. In all of the changes that she had seen, only one still remained heavy on her heart.

She and Alyks had gone on to have three more children, all sons. Alyks had been a wonderful husband, father and ruler in his lifetime. She had watched him age, powerless to stop it. His black hair had turned grey and his skin began to wrinkle. It felt like she had only just blinked and he was an old man. While she remained forever young, her love aged before her eyes. He would often stare at her and remember the young man he had once been. A fearless, impetuous man who had loved her despite the rage that consumed her. As he lay dying, he had tried to make her promise she would love again. She refused, knowing she would only ever love him. Even as he neared death, she would not placate him with lies. After Alyks, one by one her sons died, leaving only grandchildren to remind her of the life she had once had. As more children were born, she noticed only males were ever born to their bloodline. Not once was a female ever born to them, except for Gaea. Amme often wondered through the centuries how their daughter fared? Gaea had been handed over to Sisue when she was only a week old. Amme had traded her fate, for that of her daughters.

She looked at the portrait of Alyks that still hung in the great hall. She felt the hot sting of tears as she looked at him and willed her tears away. The crowned parted as the doors opened and her grandson walked into the room. He was with his wife and he carried their newborn son. He beamed with pride as he walked towards his grandmother, Queen Amme. She saw the baby's head was full of jet-black hair, as were all males in their family. She was always comforted that a part of Alyks lived on, no matter how long he had been gone.

Her grandson climbed the stairs to the throne and placed the baby in Amme's arms. She looked down at the tiny face and smiled, this baby was a reminder that life would always go on.

"Grandmother, may I present to you, Elijah." the young man said and bowed respectfully

Amme reached down and touched his little hand. His frail fingers gripped one her fingers tightly and she gave a small laugh. This one was strong like his grandfather. She stood up with him and looked directly at the crowd.

"It is my honor to present the newest prince of Thelry." she said and turned so the crowd could see the baby "You may all bow down to prince Elijah." she commanded

The crowd instantly bowed to the baby, until she finally handed him back to his father. She followed him down the steps to mingle with the crowd who had come to see their newest prince.

As she walked among the crowd, she heard her grandson's wife whispering to him loudly "I don't know why she bothers to give any of you royal titles! It is not like you will ever become king." she said snidely as she handed the baby off to the nanny.

Amme felt her blood boil at the insolent words. She made

her way towards them, as her grandson rebuked his wife "Watch your words carefully, they border on treason." he reminded her

She opened her mouth to reply, but Amme was already upon them.

She plastered a fake smile on her face and stammered "Thank you for a wonderful party, Queen Amme." she said unnerved by the look on Amme's face

Amme eyed the girl up and down in disgust, before replying "Do you mean the party for your son, who will never be king?" she asked coldly

"I meant no disrespect." the girl said nervously

Amme became enraged at the lie "You would lie to me now?" she asked through clenched teeth

"Forgive her grandmother, she is simply overwhelmed by the splendor of the day." her grandson begged

She turned to gaze at him for a moment "Do not make excuses or apologies for this woman's words. You have no control over her thoughts or her tongue. The sooner you realize this, the happier you will be." she hissed at him, before turning back to his wife

"I have been Queen of Thelry for ten thousand years. I have seen this galaxy through wars and famine. I have guided it through regime changes and brought free use of magic back for all. During that time, I have kept every generation of my family safe and fully ensconced in their royal titles. Your husband and son may never become kings, you vapid fool, but they will be kept safe. For that alone you should be grateful! You are the fourth daughter of a Duke and your birth order alone should never have allowed you such a fine marriage. You should be living on some country estate, with only a handful of servants. Instead, you live in the palace of the oldest royal family in the galaxy. You are surrounded by luxuries; you do not deserve. Yet, you do not find yourself grateful, only bitter because you will never be a queen." she said and leaned closer to the young woman's face until they were only a breath apart "You have neither the intelligence or the fortitude to ever be Queen of Thelry." she finished

Amme then stood up straight and pulled her dress down to straighten it. She took one last look at the girl, who was truly frightened now. She nodded to her grandson, before turning back to the crowd with a smile. She mingled for only a few more minutes, before signaling to her ladies, she was ready to leave. She left the party, relieved to be done.

Back in her rooms she sank into a chair. She was weary of this place again. How many wives had she seen like this one? They would marry her grandsons, but soon realize they would never ascend the throne. Amme was fae and her lifetime seemed eternal to them all. So, they would begin to plot to take the throne. Amme could no longer count, how many of them had been punished for treason.

She dismissed all of her ladies, except one. Noni, was the head of her ladies and Amme's closest friend. All of her ladies were chosen at birth from Nocri and trained in her service. A coven of witches, once meant to protect her. Her mother had chosen the first coven and she still remembered Cyni and the others fondly. Every fifty years the women would be switched out, Amme had loved them all. Most importantly, she had trusted them all.

Noni sat a cup of tea in front of her "Is the new mother causing problems already?" she asked as she sat down across from Amme

Amme nodded as she reached for the cup "Yes." she sighed "It seems like these young women can never accept their true fate. It is maddening to me Noni!" she exclaimed and took a sip of her tea "If it were a terrible fate I might understand, but it is not. None of them are meant to marry princes, but I have allowed all of my grandsons to choose freely, who they love. They and their children are given the best of everything. Their children are afforded the finest educations and may choose what field they want for their interests. What more could a wife and mother want?" she asked incredulously

Noni shook her head, unable to understand either "It is a question I cannot answer."

"Yet it continues to happen over and over." Amme said

"Would you like us to keep watch over her?" Noni asked

Amme sighed deeply in resignation at the suggestion "I suppose we must. I hate spying in my own home, but I see no other choice." she answered

"Shall I draw you a bath?" Noni asked standing up

Amme looked at her and shook her head "No, have my ship readied for me."

Noni nodded in understanding "Shall I inform prince Frederick of your absence?" she asked

Amme stood up "I will tell him myself, before I leave." she said

Amme knocked softly on the door and a voice called out "Enter." she opened the door and saw the old man sitting by the fire. He grabbed his cane so he could stand up and greet her, but she waved him back down in the chair. Frederick was her oldest living grandson and ruled in her absence. He was great grandfather to their newest prince Elijah; she had just held today.

"No, need to get up Frederick, I will join you." she said as she crossed the room towards him

As she took the chair opposite from him, he smiled at her "How were the festivities today?" he asked

Amme frowned at the memory "I am afraid our newest prince's mother may become a problem." she told him

Frederick looked at his grandmother and sighed. She sat before him unchanged by time. A young beautiful queen, who never aged with the rest of them. The generations of her grandchildren were so many, no one could even count anymore. So, they all just called her grandmother, which was ridiculous, given the way she looked. She could never understand how any of them could feel ambition. She had long ago forgotten what it felt like to be young and to want to chase your dreams. Sometimes, he even wondered if she even had dreams anymore.

"I always say you cannot tame a young heart." he finally answered

"I do seek to tame her, only to keep her intentions contained." She informed him

Frederick laughed softly at the idea "You destroyed an entire planet when you were younger than her. You brought down an empire that had reigned for five hundred years. Then you seized the power of that empire and have never let go." he reminded her

"I did it so that my children would have a better future, then the one fate had designed for them." she told him

"That is all this young mother desires, also." he countered

Now it was Amme's turn to laugh "She desires for her husband and son to become king one day. I desired for my children to be allowed to live without suffering. It is a remarkable difference of ambition." she told him

Frederick simply shrugged "I am not saying it is right. I am only saying the intention remains the same."

"I'm beginning to wonder if your mind is starting to slip, as you age." She said rudely

Frederick raised an eyebrow at her "I am only sixty-eight grandmother. My mind remains sound, it is only my opinion you do not like." he replied keeping his patience

She eyed him a moment before replying "That was rude of me, I apologize." she finally said

He waved off her apology "No apology is necessary grandmother. We all know you are far too serious, your spark left you long ago."

"My spark?" she questioned

"Yes, your spark for life. The spark that makes us all seek life and all of its joy. I suspect it died with your husband, but it could have gone out long before that." he answered

Amme just stared at him. She knew this spark he spoke of, died in her the day she handed over Gaea to Sisue. Gaea was her secret though; she had given her up to keep her safe. She would not reveal her now. Only Alyks had known she existed and only he had understood her pain. A pain they shared, until he left her alone with it. Even now as she recalled the memory, the pain had not dulled in her.

Amme stood up "I'm leaving for a few days, as always you are in charge while I am gone." she informed him

"Will you ever tell me where you go, when you leave like this?" he asked curiously

Amme left often and never had she told anyone where she went. She did not think she would start revealing her secrets today.

"I go to the place where my spark died so long ago." she said and left the room

CHAPTER 2

Amme sat in the ship and in the cold, silent darkness considered Frederick's words. She knew the joy of life had left her long ago. Some days she felt the emptiness of it inside of her like a deep hole. She would often close her eyes and think of the night when she had danced among the fountains with Alyks. Even then darkness had filled her soul. The deep rage for the Emperor, who had torn away everything she had ever loved. Alyks had seen it and it was like a mirror reflecting his own darkness, back at him. In the midst of the chaos, they had fallen in love. Their darkness was to them, what romance was to others. They could have written sonnets about it. He had begun to soften as he aged, while she had only grown harder. She knew too soon; she would have to carry on without him. He was her strength, when she felt weak. Once he was gone, she could not allow herself to feel weakness again. Instead, all she ever felt now was alone. Alone with an emptiness that threatened to overwhelm her if she didn't fight it. The problem was she didn't know how much longer she could fight it,

She saw the planet Fae in the distance and exhaled deeply. Only there, on the empty planet did she feel connected to something. It did not matter to her that the something she felt connected to, was nothing more than a long dead memory.

As she landed in the clearing of the meadow, she saw the tower. She had built the tower in the exact same spot, where Sisue's temple had once stood. Secretly, she had hoped that one day Sisue would return and bring her daughter home. She wanted her daughter to have a home here, if she ever came. She often wondered what her daughter would look like now. Was she lithe with dark hair like her father or did she favor Amme's looks? Was she happy? What were her dreams? Did she know who her parents were, or did she think Sisue was her mother?

She thought of all of these questions as she climbed the long spiral staircase, to the top of the tower. When she opened the door and finally stepped on to the flat rooftop of the tower, she would feel peace. It was only for a brief moment, but she savored it nonetheless.

She would walk to the large throne that sat in the middle of the rooftop and sink into it. It was only here on this empty planet that she would let her grief wash over her. Like a tidal wave, she would let it consume her and the tears would flow. Even the dark energy would push itself away from her and let her heart purge the grief it had bottled up. She would sit like this for days, until finally it was gone. A lonely dark fae, crying on an empty planet.

She had watched the sun rise and set three times, as she cried. Looking out over the empty landscape, where the people of Fae had once lived. It had continued to sit empty during her reign and she had refused to ever let anyone come here. She had claimed the planet as the property of Thelry. Kings had begged for centuries to be allowed to explore here, but she had always refused. Their bloodlines had once waged a war against the people of this planet, her own people had been killed into very near extinction. They would never be allowed to spoil this place again. They would never look upon the beauty, they had once destroyed.

She surveyed the landscape around her and that's when she noticed something strange. In the distance, two men were walking towards her across the meadow. Amme blinked trying to clear the vision, her eyes not believing what they were seeing. Not once, in ten thousand years, had anyone been here, but her.

The two men strolled casually and one of them even waved his arm over his head at her in a friendly greeting. She walked to the edge of the platform for a closer look. As they got closer, she noticed they were identical in every way, but one. One was clean shaven, while the other had an intricately lined beard.

When they finally reached the bottom of the tower the clean shaven one looked up at her and yelled "We are coming up." then did not bother to wait for her to agree

Amme stood in shock and continued to stare down, even after they were out of sight. She finally gave up and walked back to her throne to wait for them to come through the door.

As she waited, she began to wonder where they had come from and how they had gotten here. Perhaps, she reasoned their ship had somehow crashed here. She could think of no other explanation. They must have seen her ship land and it had days for them to reach her. She felt the dark energy inside of her begin to whisper to her in warning, to be careful of them. She flicked a wrist and two chairs appeared for them to sit in. She was not afraid of two men on an empty planet, no one was more powerful than her, she whispered back. She heard the door open behind her and the two men walked silently to the chairs.

The clean shaven one sunk down into his chair and exhaled loudly, like he was exhausted. The bearded one sat down less dramatically and folded his hands into his lap. The clean shaven one looked down at the landscape below and whistled in amazement.

He looked at Amme and said "Well, this place has certainly changed since the last time we were here! A bustling city once filled this valley and a temple sat on this very spot." he told her

"Who are you?" Amme asked ignoring his history lesson

"Forgive our rudeness!" he said "I am Cree and this is

Caspian." he said and smiled broadly at her

Amme looked at the grinning fool, unnerved by him somehow and then turned her eyes towards his brother. Caspian sat expressionless and stared back at her.

"How did you get here?" she said turning back to Cree

"Through our doorway." he replied casually

"Are you fae?" she asked astounded since she had never seen anyone else be able to call in a doorway

"No, we are the soul collectors." Caspian answered, speaking for the first time

"He makes it sound so ominous!" Cree exclaimed lightly, but shot his brother a dirty look "We are the finders of lost and rare things. Lost souls are just one of the many things we find." he explained

"How can a soul become lost?" Amme asked suspiciously

"Many different ways. It can be lost at death or in a time loop for example." Cree explained

"Or it can be given away." Caspian said coldly

"You must forgive my brother; his social skills can be terribly lacking. I am it is the fault of our Creator, whose own social skills are lacking." Cree said trying to divert the conversation back to him

Amme's eyebrows furrowed in confusion "Who is your Creator?" she asked

"The same as your own." Caspian replied vaguely

"Stop it Caspian!" Cree yelled at him angrily "You do nothing but confuse her with your riddles."

"I am afraid you are correct, I'm very confused." Amme admitted

"No worries, dark fae, everything will be explained to you." Cree reassured her

"How do you know what I am?" she asked shocked by his knowledge

Cree leaned back and looked deeply into her eyes "I can see the darkness that settled into your soul long ago. You chose it when your powers were sung in. Most fae who chose the dark energy went mad from it, but I see you live in harmony with your own. Not an easy feat for a fae."

"How can you know these things?" Amme asked breathlessly

Cree smiled at her again "It is why we were created, dark fae. To seek out a soul, one must be capable of looking into them. A glimpse into what we ourselves do not possess."

"You must have a soul!" Amme exclaimed

Cree shook his head sadly "Neither heart nor soul do we possess. Let your dark energy reach out to us and you will see. You will find nothing but an empty void where our souls should be."

"Why would you be created this way?" Amme asked sickened by the idea of a soulless creature

"We were created to serve life. A soul could only hinder our abilities." Caspian explained

"How could having a soul hinder you?" Amme asked him

"It would make us connect with you, with all of you. That is not our purpose, we are only meant to serve you and your desires. If we had souls, we would soon have our own desires and we are not meant to have our own." Cree tried to explain

"Who do you serve?" Amme asked

"Anyone who asks." Cree shrugged "Take for example a young fae who lived her long ago. She desired a man who would be her truest love and soon after she asked, a ship crashed here. The rest as they say, is history."

"Do you speak of Xirdneh, Sisue's daughter?" Amme asked becoming concerned

"That is exactly who he speaks of." Caspian confirmed

"That crash is exactly what started the Great War." Amme said shocked by the revelation

Cree shrugged and held up his hands "I do not control the outcome. I simply found the soul she desired." he said innocently

"Be careful what you wish for." Caspian warned

Amme sat back to contemplate everything she had just learned. The dark energy began buzzing around inside of her warning her to proceed carefully.

"Why are you here now?" she finally asked

"We are here seeking your soul, dark fae." Cree told her

"For what?" she asked suspiciously

"To ask a simple favor." Cree said

"Why would either of you need a favor from me?" she asked

"Because in exchange we will do a favor for you." Cree offered

"You have only to name your price dark fae and we will

do it. Would you like us to find the reborn soul of your beloved husband?" he asked

"Perhaps, you seek more power or even something your hidden heart desires?" Cree said

"What would you know of my secret heart?" Amme asked amused at his audacity

"We know that is place where you keep Gaea hidden." Caspian replied casually

Amme looked at him shocked, but before she could say anything Cree spoke "You could see her, Amme. See the woman she has become. She would never even have to know. All of your questions would finally be answered." he said soothingly

"What would you have me do in return?" she asked, blinded by the thought of Gaea

"You have only to dance the kings dance for us and I will grant your wish." Caspian answered cruelly

Amme stared at him angrily, knowing the kings dance was meant for seduction "I dance for no man." she replied enraged at the suggestion

"Your dignity is steep a price to pay for your daughter?" he asked unmoved by her anger

"Enough Caspian!" Cree yelled and his rage crossed his faced for only a moment, but Amme had seen it. She thought even at her darkest, her own rage had never matched the ferocity of his.

Cree's face was calm when he turned back to Amme "A simple favor is all we ask in return." he told her

"What is this simple favor you seek from me?" she asked

"As you know Primis has created a new species on Huma."

he began

Amme nodded "I granted him permission to do his experiments and research long ago. I hear the humans have great potential and have advanced quickly under his guidance. I have never met one though, the humans do not interest me." she told him

"They are a remarkable species, capable of a great many things. I must admit that when the Lagorian first approached me with the idea, I was skeptical." Cree confided

"So you helped him?' Amme asked

Cree nodded enthusiastically "Yes, to create the new species he needed something very rare. I helped him to secure it."

"What did he need?" Amme asked curiously

"Chaos." Caspian whispered fiercely

Cree threw his hands up again in defeat "I'm afraid that I cannot disclose. The same will apply to your secret. No matter what you ask for I will never tell another soul as long as you live." Cree swore

"So, what is it exactly you want from me?" she asked

"The humans are building a new device, but they lack a certain mineral to make it work. In all of the galaxy, the planet Fae is the only place to find it. They need your permission to come here and mine for it." Cree said, making it sound simple enough

"You want me to let them mine this planet?" she laughed

"Only a tiny amount is needed. Your mountains are full of it, they would be here less than two weeks. Little equipment is needed and only twelve men would come. They will be in and out before you even notice." Cree explained

"That is, it? That is all you ask for?" she asked skeptically

"Yes, and if you agree I will find one thing for you. I can seek out Gaea or perhaps you long to be reunited with your beloved husband. I can awaken his soul for you." Cree replied

Amme stared at him "I have seen Alyks's soul reborn many times throughout the years. A soul is meant to be awoken. A soul is not meant to live the same life again." she told him

"That is a lesson, few people ever accept dark fae." Cree told her

"That is a lesson I accepted long ago." she replied

"It would seem you are wise, dark fae. Use your wisdom to make this decision now." Caspian warned

Amme sat back and contemplated the request. The dark energy pushed at her to refuse. Yet, the idea of finally knowing what had happened to her daughter pushed at her harder. If the humans did no damage and only wanted a small amount of mineral for their weapon, what harm could there be? To see the face of her daughter and learn her fate, was a treasure she had never hoped to find.

"I will agree on two conditions." Amme told the Twins

"Name them." Cree said

"The first is that two weeks is the limit they will have on my planet. If they do not find this mineral in that time, they must leave." she said

"Agreed and the second condition?" Cree asked

"I must be present the entire time they are here. I will not allow them unattended in this place." she said

"Done." Cree said and stood up; the deal complete

He walked over to Amme and held out his hand to her "The humans may come and mine for two weeks, under your supervision. In return I will find your daughter and you may finally know her fate. Do we have a deal?" he asked

Amme placed her hand in his to shake it and a shiver went down her spine at the coldness of his touch "We have a deal." she agreed

Amme stood at the edge of the platform and watched as the Twins walked back in the direction they had come from. The cold shiver in her spine, had settled into her entire body now. The dark energy kept hissing at her "What have you done!"

When they were out of earshot of Amme, Cree turned on Caspian "What were you playing at up there? You almost ruined everything!" he accused angrily

"You pretend to be me all of the time, brother. I was simply seeing what it felt like to be you." Caspian replied unconcerned with Cree's anger

Cree laughed at him "Well you did a terrible job of it. You are such a fool Caspian! Only evil can mimic good, it doesn't work the other way around." he mocked

"I'm still going to keep trying. All you do is leave destruction in your wake. We are meant to serve life; Cree and we both know what will happen if the humans complete their weapon." Caspian pointed out

"Caspian, you are such a simple fool sometimes. We serve the story of our Creator. Death must happen for life to be reborn. The souls must cycle through so the goal can be achieved. The goal is for the souls to tell their stories, how can that happen if the story never changes? If it were left up to you nothing would ever change. You may stick to what you are good at and I will stick to what I am good at." Cree warned

"I will not let you harm her." Caspian told him

Cree shrugged "You cannot stop me brother. Besides, there will be plenty of fae for you to save in the future. Right now, our goal is to ensure the Immortals are created." he said and waved in their fiery doorway.

CHAPTER 3

The Twins stepped through their doorway onto the planet Huma. Explosions rocked the ground, but their steps never faltered. All around them chaos rained down and Cree loved it. The humans were at war with one another, yet again. When Primis had created the genetic sequencing in his lab, he could have never predicted this. He had built an entire civilization for them, while they gestated. It had been impressive with only the finest Lagorian technology. The first few generations had been crude and learned slowly, but when he enhanced their brain size their ability to learn exploded. The Twins had witnessed every new species evolution since the beginning of time. Some species took a long time to develop, while others evolved more quickly. Primis had made the mistake of interfering he thought. He recognized he had offered them too much, too soon. He would never realize his mistake was not in interfering but in creating them in the first place. Cree loved mistakes though, he thought they always afforded many wonderful opportunities.

The massive cities that Primis had built, had been reduced to nothing more than rubble. As the Twins neared the mouth of a cave, an armed battalion stepped forward to halt them. They pointed their guns at the brothers.

"State your business." One of them barked

Caspian looked at the group in disgust and raised a hand at them. The men went flying backwards with such force, every bone in their bodies broke. Caspian looked down at the bodies of the dead men and said "What a vile species they are."

Cree stepped over a body unconcerned by what Caspian had just done "Agreed." he said and walked into the cave

Bare light bulbs hung loosely to light their way, into the makeshift command center. Men in uniforms crowded around computer monitors. They tracked their progress and kept count of the dead.

A large man with bright red hair approached them smiling to see them "I hope you have good news for me?" he greeted them

Cree smiled back with the same enthusiasm and said "Indeed I do! I have found the mineral you need and have secured the rights for you to mine it." he reported

"Wonderful! Come and have a drink with me while we discuss the details." he offered and led them both to a side room

Crude chairs and tables had been set up and the man went to get glasses and a bottle.

"Where did you finally find it?" he asked as he walked back towards them with his hands full

"On the planet Fae." Cree said as a glass was set in front of him

"The planet Fae?" the man said surprised and began to fill their glasses "I thought that planet was off limits to everyone in the galaxy?' he asked

"It is, but I struck a deal with the Queen of Thelry. You have two weeks to get your mineral and get out." Cree told him and downed the glass

"Hopefully that will be enough time." the man said as he drank down his own glass

A loud explosion rocked the cave, sending debris falling

down on them "By the sounds of it, you won't hold out much longer than that anyways." Caspian said and began wiping the falling dust off the shoulders of his jacket

"We are holding our own." the man replied irritated

"There was one stipulation though." Cree told him "Queen Amme must be present while you mine on her planet. Her own ancestors once inhabited the planet and she has a certain fondness for it."

The man nodded "That should be no problem."

"What should be no problem?" another man asked as he entered the room

Everyone looked up to see who had joined them "Ian!" the man exclaimed "Look who has come to join us for a drink and deliver good news."

Ian eyed the Twins suspiciously. He had never liked the two men, although he couldn't pinpoint exactly why. They had simply shown up one day, offering to help. They had a weak explanation that Primis had sent them, but Ian doubted it. Primis had stopped coming to the planet long ago, before Ian had ever been born. Primis could stop the war if he wanted to, but he had abandoned his faithful.

Ian sat down next to the other man and poured himself a drink "What good news have they delivered, Danby?' he asked the man

"They have located the mineral we need to complete our weapon and end the war." Danby told him excitedly

"Where?" Ian asked

"On the planet Fae! The queen of Thelry has agreed to let us mine for two weeks. It should be plenty of time to get enough for the weapon." Danby told him

Ian raised an eyebrow at the news "I have heard rumors of the queen. Why would she agree to help us now, she doesn't even allow us on her planet?" Ian pointed out

"Fae is uninhabited, so you offer the people of Thelry no threat there." Cree answered reasonably

"We offer no threat to the people of Thelry, under any circumstance." Ian said offended by the statement

Caspian laughed at this "Perhaps, she feels threatened because humans have been engaging in never ending civil wars. Your species has been fighting ever since the first of you could pick up a stick."

"We have never attacked another planet or it's people. Many of our ambassadors have visited other planets without a problem. We have visited every planet in the universe, except Thelry. She will not even allow her own people to visit another planet if we are there." Ian said bitterly

"You have never attacked another planet because you are too busy attacking your own. Regardless you will meet the queen herself and perhaps, she will offer you an explanation." Caspian told him and smirked at the idea of Amme explaining herself to anyone

"Perhaps, I will ask her when I meet her." Ian told Caspian challengingly

"When do we leave?" Danby asked trying to steer away the tense conversation

"Tomorrow, you should leave early. Amme is expecting you." Cree answered "Take no more than a dozen men."

Danby looked at Ian "We should start preparing now if we expect to leave at first light." he said and Ian nodded in agreement

Cree and Caspian stood up simultaneously, their job here done for now.

"Wait!" Danby said "How do we contact you if we need anything else?" he asked them

"You don't." Caspian told him coldly "The promise made to Primis was that we would help you find the mineral to complete your weapon and end the war. Once your device is working, the war will be over."

"We will check in on you when you are on Fae, just to make sure you find what you need." Cree reassured them

The Twins started walking for the door, but Cree hesitated and turned back to the men "Tell me again what you are calling this new weapon?" he asked

"We are calling it a nuclear missile." Danby answered proudly "We will have one hundred of them to use against the enemy."

Cree smiled "What a magnificent name! I shall make sure to remember it." he said and followed Caspian out

After they had left Ian looked at Danby gravely and said "I don't trust those two."

Danby looked shocked by the admission "Why not? They have done exactly what they have promised. Can you imagine what else we might find on that uninhabited planet?" he asked excited

"It is an untapped resource, but that queen will never allow us to take anything from there." Ian said

"I'm betting she can be charmed, just like any other woman. Besides, even if she can't be charmed, once are weapons are functional, we will be a force to be reckoned with. No planet will be able to stop us! What do we always say?" Danby asked prodding Ian for the answer

"What isn't given, can always be taken." Ian said repeating the planets motto

"Exactly! While we mine, I will send a couple of men out to scout around. We will see what the planets has to offer us." Danby said excitedly

Ian stood up "Well let's go get everything ready." he said infected by Danby's good cheer

Danby stood up next to him "I will meet you at the loading dock. I want to go and check on the entrance guards, they haven't radioed in for a while."

Ian made his way through the rubble of the city, in the darkness before dawn. The world seemed so quiet and he enjoyed the peacefulness of it, even though he knew it wouldn't last. As soon as the sun rose, the fighting would begin again. He made his way down the torn-up streets and bombed out buildings. The city that he had once loved, now abandoned. Even in complete chaos he knew his way. He had grown up in this city. He remembered watching parades go by, when he was a child. The city had been magnificent, made entirely of glass and marble. Huma had vast marble veins throughout the entire planet. Even the sidewalks and streets, had been paved in marble. On sunny days the city would shine like a diamond in its brilliance.

He finally reached a bombed-out apartment building and carefully made his way to the fifth floor. When he reached the apartment, he was looking for, he saw the door hung loosely still by only one hinge. He stepped inside and a flood of memories washed over him.

A beautiful young woman, dressed only in his shirt stood at the stove. She turned to look at him and smile and his heart broke all over again. Her short, curly brown hair and matching brown eyes looking at him, while she attempted to make eggs. She had been a terrible cook, but he had eaten everything she had made him with a smile on his face. He laughed at the thought of it now. Then he looked at the spot where the window seat had once been and there she was again. She was curled up reading a book, wrapped in a soft blanket. The rain was pouring outside the window and she looked so content. He turned and walked into the bedroom and she lay on her stomach sleeping. The sheet kept the bottom half of her covered, but her bare back looked beautiful in the moonlight.

He walked to where the closet had been and sank to his knees. The memory of her overwhelmed him as he dug through the rubble. Finally, he found what he was looking for and pulled it free. As he began to wipe it off with his sleeve, tears began to flood his eyes and the last memory of her set itself free.

He was late coming home from work that day. The blast had hit the building as he had rounded the corner. People were screaming and dust filled the air so thick, it was impossible to see. He fought his way through the terrified crowd, as they scrambled everywhere to find safety. A sea of people running from the blast, kept pushing him back, but he pushed back every time. He was coughing and choking by the time he made it upstairs. The door to their apartment had been blown open and she lay on the floor inside. Her head and one arm sticking out from under the marble wall that had fallen on her, crushing her under its weight. He had screamed for what had felt like hours. He still wasn't sure. As he struggled to pull her body out from underneath the wall, his mind broke. When he had finally wrenched her free, he had sat and cradled her broken body. He rocked her gently and spoke soft words to her. Her beautiful face and hair were covered in the white dust from the blast and he wiped it away carefully. It was Danby who had finally found him like that and helped him, bring her body down.

Once long ago, she had laid in his arms and they had looked up at the night sky. It was then that she had told him she wanted to see the planet Fae someday. She thought it must be beautiful and wild. She told him she imagined it was overgrown and full of exotic flowers. Untouched by hands, only touched by nature, she had said. As he had held her broken body, he had promised her that one day he would take her there. He had promised her that he would lay her to rest there. As he dusted off the book of her favorite poetry, he thought he was finally going to fulfill his promise to her. The queen of Thelry would have to kill him, if she tried to stop him.

CHAPTER 4

As their ship flew low over the planet, towards the landing coordinates, the men all looked out the window in awe. The landscape below them was wild and untouched by man. Herds of wild animals ran free and giant flocks of birds flew beside them. The bodies of water below were crystal clear and never tainted by pollution.

"I have never seen anything like it!" Ian exclaimed in wonderment, thinking of the ruined world they had just left

"What a waste of resources! Can you imagine how many of our people could be fed from these animals?" Danby said bitterly "People on Huma starve, while food runs in wild here."

"Food!" one of the soldiers laughed "Imagine how much gold this planet has that is yet to be discovered."

"After this war is over, we will return here and begin to utilize this planet full of riches." Danby promised them all

Ian shook his head at the idea "The queen of Thelry owns this planet and I doubt she will allow us to just take it from her." he reminded them all

"She never allowed anyone on this planet before and we are the first, maybe her heart has softened. Maybe, she has heard of the dire state of our planet and our people and will agree to help us." one of the soldiers suggested

Danby laughed at the suggestion "I doubt very muvh that her heart has softened. I have heard she is as cold as stone and her will cannot be changed." he replied

"Well, something changed her mind." the soldier pointed out

"I would guess the Twins struck some sort of deal with her for the mineral." Ian said and shuddered at the thought of the Twins

"We will feel her out when we are here. She may be malleable to some sort of agreement. If not, our new weapon may help change her mind." Danby said

"Are you suggesting we try to go to war with her?" Ian asked shocked

Danby shrugged "I am simply saying, if it is not given, it can be taken." he said

Before Ian could reply one of the men pointed out the window and asked "What is that?"

They all leaned forward as the tower came into view. It was so tall, it looked as if it might touch the clouds. It was pure white and glinted in the sun. they were all shocked by the sight of it, since they had seen no other building or structures of any kind. It seemed out of place and almost ominous.

"That is where we are landing." Ian announced

Amme saw the ship approaching slowly and felt a pang of regret in her stomach at the sight of it. Had she made the right decision, letting the humans come here? She would not even allow them on Thelry and yet she welcomed them to Fae. She had kept a close eye on their progress as they developed as a species and was not impressed. Whatever Primis had set out to create, he had obviously failed miserably. She knew their planet was on the brink of dying. Like parasites, they kept consuming it and stripping it down of resources. Resources that they then fought over. They had no monarchy, instead they preferred to rule over one another. Never realizing only, the wealthy would ever thrive in this system of governing. They broke off into packs like dogs and let their alpha males decide the fate of them all. She had forbidden them to ever come to her planet, or even mingle with her people. She would not them infect her planet in any way.

When she had discovered that Primis had allowed them to believe he was a deity, she was outraged. She had stopped allowing Primis on her planet when she had found out. She truly believed the Lagorian was mad, he reminded her of the Emperor from long ago.

Yet, the Twins had offered the only thing her heart truly desired. The only thing she could not refuse and so two weeks with the humans would have to be tolerated.

She watched from the top of the tower, as they walked off their ship. They looked like tiny ants scurrying, from where she stood. She knew she would crush them like tiny ants, if they disobeyed her rules while they were here.

She finally leaned over the edge of the rooftop and called down "Your leader may come up."

They all looked up at the faint sound of her voice, but could not see here.

"Shall we?" Danby asked Ian who nodded and took a deep breath

When they opened the door at the bottom of the tower, they looked up in amazement. The spiral staircase looked like it went up for miles. Both of them groaned at the idea of climbing all of those stairs.

"I wonder how old she is?" Danby said

"She must be very old. I remember once hearing as a boy, how beautiful she was." Ian guessed

"Well, an old woman should be easy enough to charm." Danby said happily

"You better hope you're her type then." Ian quipped

Danby laughed and clapped him on the back "I am every woman's type!" he said conceitedly "Besides if I'm not, then you most certainly are, you handsome devil."

It felt like hours had passed, when they finally reached the top of the staircase. There were two doors, one to the right of them and one just above them. They knew she was on the roof, so they opened the door above them. The sunlight hit their eyes and blinded them both for a second. As their eyes adjusted, they saw her and both of them gasped.

She couldn't be any older than twenty, they both thought. They had expected an old woman. Instead, a beautiful young woman stood before them. Finally, Danby took the first step forward and Ian followed him.

"We are to meet the queen of Thelry." Danby stammered at her nervously

Amme gestured for them to sit in the chairs in front of the throne, wordlessly. She took quick stock of the two men. Almost equal in height, but very difference in appearance. One had bright red hair, cut short in military style. The other had longer dark hair, pulled back and olive skin. As they sat down, she lowered herself onto her throne. Still not saying a word to them.

"Will she be meeting us soon?' Ian asked confused

"Who?" Amme asked confused

"The queen of Thelry?" he answered

"I am the queen of Thelry." she said

The two men looked at one another in confusion and then looked back at her "You must forgive us; we were expecting someone older." Ian explained

Amme leaned back now in understanding "I forget that humans do not have magic. I can assure you both I am very old." she told them

Danby laughed at the ludicrous idea "You do not look like you will see your thirtieth birthday for a very long time still."

Amme stared at him expressionless "I saw my thirtieth birthday over ten thousand years ago. I was born long before your species was ever created." she informed him

They both sat in stunned silence for a moment "Are you like Primis then? Are you a God?" Danby asked

"Primis is more a God, then that chair you sit upon." she answered sarcastically "He is nothing more than a scientist who created you in a laboratory. You have much to learn about the true nature of the universe, unfortunately I will not be the one to teach you." she informed them "Now tell me how long it will take you to find the mineral you seek?" she asks

"We will set up our camp and start looking today. The Twins have assured us we will find it in your caves." Ian answered

"What do you call the mineral you seek?" she asked

"Azurite." Ian answered

"There is a cave system less than a mile from here. You may set up your camp below, but be mindful of this planet. I will not have it stripped the way you do your own. Take only what you need without destroying anything." she warned

"We will have to cut into the cave walls once we find the mineral." Danby told her

"Once you have found the mineral you seek, you will come and find me. This planet has seen enough destruction. I will remove it for you." She informed them

Danby looked around the landscape in confusion "This place looks like it has never been touched." he scoffed

Amme stared at him "Looks can be deceiving."

"Why do you let this place go to waste?" Danby asked boldly

Amme's eyes glared at him now "How do I let it go to waste?' she asked

"The animals could be used for food. The trees could be used to build homes. The water could be used for power. So many things here could be used for the good of others." he said passionately, thinking of all the starving people on Huma

"When you say others, do you speak of your own people?" she asked quietly

"We are one example, of course. People on our planet are dying of starvation. Our cities are in ruins and need rebuilt. I am sure there are others like ourselves." Danby answered

"Why are your people starving? Why do your cities lay in ruins?" Amme asked patiently

"War." Danby said

Amme looked at them both now "Long ago this planet also saw war. An entire race of people was almost wiped out. The few that remained left long ago. War is fought by men and it is always fought for the same reason. They want something that someone else possesses. they will enforce their own will on others, all in an attempt to get the thing they want. I could feed your starving. You could down every tree here and rebuild your cities. You could drain every drop of water from this place, but do you know what would happen?" she asked them

"What?" Ian asked intrigued with how her mind worked

"You would simply destroy it all again. Until you learn how to stop fighting wars, your problems will never change. This planet is not going to waste, it is simply waiting for a species that will appreciate it." she said and shrugged

"All species wage war." Danby pointed out

Amme swung her gaze to him "Then it will sit empty for eternity." she informed him

Ian stood up when he saw Danby's murderous glare at the answer he received "We should get started! We have a lot to do." he reminded Danby

Danby stood up in frustration "Yes, we should go." he said through clenched teeth

Amme simply nodded to them both, but remained seated. They began the long walk down the stairs in silence. Halfway down, Ian started to laugh.

"What's so funny?" Danby asked still seething in anger

"I guess we know now, that not all women find you charming." he said and burst out laughing again

Amme sat on her throne fuming. What game were the Twins playing at with her? She knew the soul collectors must have known, before they even came here to ask her to make a deal. It was their business to know and even she had known the moment she had laid eyes on him. Ian was Alyks's soul reborn. It was unmistakable and unforgivable. She never allowed his soul in such close proximity to her. It would be too easy for him to

SHAWNA BENNETT

awaken.

CHAPTER 5

She watched them scurrying around below. They were setting up their camp and rationing their food supply. They collected wood to build a fire. She sighed heavily at the sight of Ian.

She had seen Alyks's soul reborn many times. She always kept her distance from him. She knew he would be drawn to her, but she kept him protected. No one had ever told her a soul must not be awoken, but deep inside she knew the truth of it. She couldn't imagine how devastated he would be to find her this way. Her appearance had not changed, but she knew her soul had. At first, she had only used the darkness as an escape. Only calling on it when her sorrow became too much to contain. Slowly, she had begun letting it stay longer and longer. Letting it numb her, until it had become her constant companion. It had dulled her pain, but in return it had hardened her heart. She could not remember the last time she had felt an emotion besides the sorrow that lingered.

When she was with Alyks's he had tempered her sorrow, with hope. Now a rage consumed her, that even the dark energy strained to hold back in her. She was no longer the girl he had met long ago. To find her this way would only ruin him if he was awoken.

The Twins, of course, would have known they sent his soul here. They were tricksters and she had underestimated them. She thought back to their conversation and realized to late, Caspian had been trying to warn her. She would be wary of them in the future, especially Cree. If he thought he could best her, he had played his hand to early. She would ensure that he would not know the hand she held in this game. Her father's words echoed to her now, you cannot stop, what you cannot see.

Ian wiped the sweat off his brow with the back of his hand. As he looked up, he saw the queen staring down at them. He felt like he knew her somehow, but that was impossible. He had never met her before, still he could not shake the feeling. He shook his head at his own madness and blamed it on the heat. He needed to focus on why they were here. They needed to find the azurite and complete their weapon. Once they used the weapon, the war would be over and they could begin to rebuild their world. A world that was finally free of inbred humans. A world free of magic.

Night settled in on them quickly. Fires were lit and plans made for the next day. Two groups would go in search of the caves. The scientists they had brought along would test the samples they gathered all throughout the night. Some of the men went to bed for the night, while others sat and played cards. Ian and Danby sat by the fire alone, drinking.

"What did you think of the queen of Thelry?" Ian finally asked breaking the silence

"I think she is an unnatural abomination. It is magic that keeps her looking so young. I would not be surprised to find she drinks the blood of children, to keep her youth." he said in disgust

"That is a heavy accusation!" Ian said surprised at the venom in his voice "Primis never ages either." he pointed out

"Primis is a God. I don't care what blasphemy that witch would have us believe." he said and spit on the ground next to him "Do not forget where your loyalty lies, Ian." he warned

"My loyalty always has been and always will be to the Alliance. I do not need a reminder from you, Danby. If I ever forget the thought of my wife's dead body serves as the only reminder I will ever need." he said angrily

Danby nodded at him and stared into the fire. Magic had started this war and they intended to wipe it out. The universe was thick with it though and when they cleansed Huma, they would start a new campaign. The Alliance had dedicated themselves to its eradication long ago.

When the humans had first conquered space travel, they had thought it was a marvelous feat. At first, they had visited new planets and new species with enthusiasm. They had once stood in awe of the technology of Cala. They had been brought to tears by the music of the Aegerthians. For centuries it had been beneficial to them, until the children had begun to be born. When the humans had begun to mate with people on other planets, the half breeds were born. Children of humans, who possessed magical abilities. These children grew into adults, they knew they had a problem. Two separate factions emerged from this and the Alliance had been formed to stop magic.

One day a child had been born among them, that would start the war on Huma. Her name was Miori and as she grew, so did her power. Primis had called the ability telekinesis and had warned in his ancient writings about the use of it. The Alliance, simply called it a threat. As Miori grew, she was not content to accept the fate of her own kind. Half breeds could only hold menial jobs and could never be declared citizens. They were given private encampments to live so they could not infect the citizens with their magic. They were barely given enough food to survive, but their survival concerned no one that mattered. It was Miori who rallied them together and told them they did not have to accept this fate. At first it began as peaceful protests that the humans ignored.

One day as they marched through the streets, violence erupted from them. Soldiers were sent in, as the humans had grown tired of their workforce not showing up. Bathrooms were not being cleaned and an entire field of crops had begun to rot. The humans had lost patience for a cause, they did not believe in.

It had started with no warning. Miori walked next to an old man. He was unsteady on his feet, so she gripped his arm as they walked. He had been born in the camps long ago. His mother was human and his father was from Riffin. He had spent his life in servitude, simply because he had the gift of sight. As he shambled along a vision came to him and he stopped.

"What's wrong?" Miori asked him

He looked into her face terrified "Something terrible is coming to this place Miori, you have to leave." he warned her

"What is coming?" she asked, but before he could even answer a soldier came up to him

"Keep moving!" the soldier yelled at them both

A single tear fell down the old man's face when he saw the face of the soldier, but he did not move. His fate had come for him at last. The soldier took the butt of his gun and slammed it into the old man's face. It felt as if everything were happening in slow motion, as Miori watched his face shatter from the blow. As he crumpled to the ground, Miori felt the power inside of her begin to grow. As she slowly drew in her breath, she felt it fill her with energy. As she screamed out in horror at the sight before her, a rush of energy was expelled from her body. That scream knocked everyone backwards with the force of a bomb. The crowd was thrown everywhere as the buildings began collapsing all around them. Chaos erupted and suddenly more magic was being used. Miori stood completely still in the middle of all of the destruction and watched as her own people began using their magic for the first time. The time had come for war, as she knew it always would. This is the incident that triggered the war they now all fought. This was also the day, that Ian's wife had died. Crushed in the rubble of their apartment building, waiting for him to come home. Danby knew, Ian needed no reminders of why he fought against magic. The thought of his wife would keep him fighting, until his dying day. Even now when the half breeds seemed to winning the war, he knew Ian would never stop. Danby stared into the fire and wondered what would have happened if he had not hit the old man with his gun that day?

As the sun began to peek over the clouds, Ian realized the fire had gone out long ago. Danby's chair sat empty next to him and he stood up and stretched. His muscles tight from having spent all night in the chair. He stretched his arms above his head. He had become so mesmerized by the moons last night. The moon on Huma was a brilliant white, but the two moons above Fae glowed in a beautiful silver. He knew he must begin to look for the perfect place to lay his wife to rest. She would have loved the moons on this planet.

Amme had sat up and watched him all night. Every time he had come here Alyks would stare up at the moons. He had told her once that it brought him comfort. He knew that wherever Sisue had taken Gaea, she would tell her about the moons of Fae. He liked to imagine that Gaea would close her eyes to imagine them and thought about him when she did. He had loved his three sons with all of his heart, but his daughter was the missing piece of it.

Amme preferred the sun to remember Gaea by, it glowed the same way her daughter had. As she crested the top of the hill, the first rays of it began to shine through. She closed her eyes and felt the warmth of it on her face. Like tiny warm fingers reaching out to her, to reassure her that Gaea was fine. She remembered the golden light that Gaea was bathed in, the life force Sisue had called it. The energy that surrounded them all, but few could touch. Amme felt it on her face now and knew in her heart that the life force was love.

"Beautiful, isn't it?" a voice called form behind her

She turned to see Ian as he came to stand next to her "You shouldn't be here." she said quietly turning her gaze away from him

"Why not?" he asked innocently

Amme opened her mouth to say something, but could think of no real answer. So, she closed her mouth and simply shrugged.

"Does it ever get boring?" Ian asked her

Amme was confused by the question "Does what, ever get boring?' she asked

"Sunrises or sunsets? Life in general I guess, since you have lived so long. It seems like everything would lose its fascination after a while." he answered

"It becomes less surprising I suppose. Everything has a way of repeating itself, but every once in a while, something amazing happens. Not with people of course, they never change, but with other things." she said

"Like what?" he asked curiously

"A new flower will appear, seemingly out of nowhere. A song will be sung that has never been heard before. A new animal will suddenly come into existence. Little things like that, that usually go unnoticed." she explained

"Maybe those things have always existed and you just never noticed before." he argued

Maybe, but perhaps someone imagines them into existence. You do not have to believe a thing for it to be true. The universe is filled with mysteries that will never be explained to any of us. All I know is that every once in a while, something new appears and I have no idea where it came from." she told him

"I'm sure the answers are out there for those who seek them." he said

"Not all questions can be answered. If I have learned anything in my long life, that is the most valuable." she told him

"Well, I better get back to camp, we don't have time to waste." he said and turned to walk back down the hill

In the distance Amme saw a fiery doorway appear and felt a surge of anger. She turned now also, to prepare for the arrival of the Twins.

The Twins caught the group of men, as they were heading out to search for the caves. Danby smiled in greeting; he was always happy to see Cree. Ian on the other hand, groaned inwardly. He knew that Primis had sent them to help, but something always felt off with these two. He didn't know why he felt this way, no one else around him seemed to notice.

"Have you come to help?" Danby asked them enthusiastically

"We have done all we can, my friend. We do not interfere in the lives of men." Cree said apologetically and Caspian burst into laughter

The sound of Caspian's laughter caught both of them off guard "Apologies, my brother is right! We are the servants of life." he said good naturedly

Cree clapped his brother on the shoulder and gave it a squeeze in warning.

Ian looked at them both uncomfortably and decided to change the subject "The queen is not what we were expecting."

he told them

Cree glanced up to the top of the tower, but did not see her "The queen is a very rare thing indeed." he said looking back at the men

"How is she rare?" Danby asked curiously

"She is the last of her kind." Caspian answered

"What is her kind?" Ian asked

"She is the only dark fae, still in existence." Cree told them and saw their confusion "The people of fae, once were among the most powerful beings in the universe. In each of the females was the power of all magic. When they were the proper age, the fae would gather and sing to the life force to gift them with their full power. The fae believed in the goodness of the life force, so most were gifted with the silver light. A small few of them were gifted by the dark energy. The dark energy is the power of destruction, those were the fae to be feared. Those are the fae, that eventually let the darkness consume them completely. When it does, they are unstoppable and the queen is the last one." he explained

Ian gasped "She does not seem dark." he said stunned

Cree shook his head "Be wary of her." he warned "The dark fae are masters at seduction, by the time you trust her it will be too late to save your soul."

"How is she allowed to be queen?" Danby asked angrily

"How can she be stopped? She has already destroyed and entire planet and its people." Cree told them conspiratorially

"You have no worries though, your own God Primis keeps you safe." Caspian told them sarcastically

Both men sighed in relief, not catching the sarcasm.

"You better hurry along, you haven't much time." Cree said and shooed them away

Amme sat at the top of the tower and waited for the Twins. She finally saw the humans heading for the caves and knew they would appear soon. She stood in front of the door and waited.

As they stepped through the door, Cree noticed the red dress she wore. He eyed the beautiful woman up and down, not bothering to hide his lust.

"Has anyone ever told you how beautiful you are queen Amme?" he asked

She kept the look of disgust from her face and answered "Many times."

"I believe if I had a heart, I would fall madly in love with you." he told her flirtatiously

"I believe if you had a heart, I would have already ripped it from your chest for speaking to me like that." she informed him boldly and turned to walk to her throne as Caspian burst out laughing again

Cree sat down across from her and smiled pleasantly at her, while he stretched out like a cat. Caspian sat down stiffly and did not move. They both waited patiently for Cree to be still.

"What do you think of the humans?" Cree finally asked when he had gotten comfortable

"I have only met two of them, but I remain unimpressed." she reported

"You must look harder than!" he exclaimed "They are a remarkable species. I am impressed that Primis was able to cook up such a complex species in his lab." he told her

"They have never stopped waging war on one another since their creation. How are they remarkable, they are worse than dogs with their fighting? At least a dog can become an alpha." Amme asked

"All species have seen war. Even you Amme." Caspian said

"Yes, but theirs is never ending. They have never known peace." she argued

"Do you know why they fight now?" Cree asked

Amme simply shrugged her shoulders, not even bothering to try to guess.

"Magic!" Cree said excitedly and Amme's brows furrowed in confusion "Some of them have developed magical abilities, while most have not. The two sides fight to either save or destroy those who have it." he explained

"So, the humans you have brought here, fight to save magic?" she asked

Cree leaned forward and said seriously "They are willing to die for what they believe in." he answered and Amme did not realize he hadn't actually answered her question

"I do not know why anyone would fight against magic. It develops in every species, to go against that is to go against creation." she said

"Are you ready for news of your daughter?" he asked before she could realize his deception

"Yes." she said nervously

Amme could not understand why she suddenly felt so nervous, to hear news of her. It is all that she had thought about since the day long ago, when she handed her to Sisue.

"She is well." Cree said "She has dedicated her life to the

sciences, even though she is gifted with extraordinary power, like Sisue. Gaea can harness the life force and uses it in her studies." he told her

Amme nodded and felt her throat tighten, as the tears began to slide down her cheeks "She is why I chose the dark energy, so that she could have that fate." Amme said

"A wise choice indeed." Cree complimented hr

"Have you seen her?" Amme asked wondering if she would finally see her daughters face

Caspian shook his head "Not yet, she is in a different realm. We go there next." he reassured her

"Where?" Amme asked

"She is on a planet that she herself created. It is called Earth." Caspian told her

"She created a planet?" Amme asked in awe

"The life force is very strong in your daughter. You should be proud." Cree told her

"I did not know she would have the power of creation." Amme admitted

"Sisue taught her well. We are told she is experimenting with large animals there." Caspian reported

Cree shook his head enthusiastically "Dinosaurs are what she is calling them, I believe. I am curious to see them." Cree chimed in

They both stood up simultaneously "We must go. The next time you see us, you will also see your daughter's face." Cree told her

"That I look forward to." Amme said almost wistfully

As the Twins walked back towards their doorway Caspian asked Cree "Why did you lie to her about which side the humans fight for?"

"I didn't, she merely heard exactly what she wanted to hear. Besides, she lied to us about Ian." he said

"How did she lie? She never said a word." Caspian argued

"She did not mention that she knew and an omission is a lie. She knows Ian houses her dead husband's soul. I could feel her rage at me for it." Cree said

"Why do you think she keeps that hidden?" Caspian asked

"Because she is a worthy opponent in this game we play, brother!" he said happily "She is no match for me of course, but she at least plays the game. Everything is going according to plan."

"What is the plan?" Caspian asked, knowing he could never figure out what direction Cree wanted things to go

"You'll see." Cree said cryptically

Caspian had never been able to guess the outcome of any of Cree's deals. He simply stood by and watched as Cree manipulated every situation around him. How did the humans and the dark fae have anything to do with Primis? How did Gaea factor into his plan? One thing Caspian knew for certain, was that everyone had a role to play in his schemes. When Cree made a deal all those around him were destroyed. Each time it happened Caspian felt himself grow weaker, while Cree grew stronger. Everything must exist in pairs; the Source had once told him. He must hold on, before Cree was the only thing that continued to exist.

CHAPTER 6

Amme felt conflicted after the Twins had left. She had never wanted to become involved with the humans and their problems. Alyks's soul had of course, chosen to fight to save magic. He had been gifted the ability to conjure. She remembered the night he had set off fireworks as they danced. She then remembered the first time his lips had touched hers; they were soft and yet firm. He didn't tell her she was beautiful and try to win her with charm. Instead, he opened the most secret place in his heart and allowed her to do the same. Alyks had been the only person to see the true ugliness inside of her and love her despite it. He loved the parts of her that everyone else hated. He had loved her stubbornness and anger. He stood by her side without question or hesitation. He would know even now, why she never tried to awaken his soul. She would never let him suffer the loss of their daughter again. Forgetting was a kindness. It was because she loved him that she would never let him suffer again. She had seen his soul many times throughout the centuries and many times longed for him to hold her once more.

One time in particular had been the hardest. He had come with a diplomatic envoy from Cala. He had looked exactly the same and it took her breath away. Her prince from Cala had returned to her. One night he had caught her outside while she was staring at the ocean. He had stopped to talk to her and it had brought to mind their first night together. She had become so swept up in the moment, she had almost kissed him. As he had leaned in to kiss her, he whispered "It feels like we have met before......perhaps in another life." in that split second before his lips touched hers, she knew! She knew that if they kissed his soul would awaken and the dark energy hissed at her to stop. It warned that souls must never be awoken to their old lives. She had pushed him back and called for her guards, as he begged for an explanation. She had banished him from her planet and wept as his ship left. He was the only comfort she had known since she had become a dark fae and she still didn't know how to live without him. She had kept a wide berth from his reborn soul since then. She always recognized it and never allowed him to be near her.

Now he was right next to her and would be for two weeks. She vowed to keep her distance, but she also had one other love in her heart. If she got a picture of Gaea, she would show it to him. He would not understand it now, but when his soul went to rest in the heavens he would understand. When Alyks went to rest in the heavens above Lagoria, he would finally know the face of his daughter.

Ian and Danby led the group into the caves. Amme had been right; it had been easy enough to find. About four hundred feet into the opening, it forked into two directions and each team set off in opposite directions.

"Do you know what we are even looking for?" Danby asked Ian as they began to pick ax into a cave wall

"Cree said it is a deep blue mineral, so look for blue." Ian replied

"We are sure this is all we need to make the weapon work?" Danby asked concerned

Ian stopped stabbing at the wall and looked at Danby irritated "I don't know!" he exclaimed "Primis has not been to Huma in centuries, but the Twins insist he sent them to help us. I only know what I have been told the same as you."

"You sound as if you are losing your faith in Primis." Danby said pointing out his blasphemous tone

"I question my faith the same way all men do! Why did our Creator spend so much time with our ancestors, only to disappear on us? We put our faith in a being we have never seen with our own eyes. Our prayers go unanswered as people around us die." Ian admitted

"Yet, we fight a holy war!" Danby argued "The main rule we were given by Primis, was no human shall practice magic. Our creator knew how dangerous it could be and forbid from us. Primis knew it would lead to our destruction and he was right. Look how easily the half breeds have taken over our planet, using magic. If they are not stopped pure humans will cease to exist. We allowed the half breeds to live among us, when we should have eradicated them at birth. Primis could see what would happen, before we ever did. We must live by the words and laws he left us. Now more than ever it is crucial to our survival."

Ian shook his head in defeat, Danby was a zealot and could not think with reason "I know all of this Danby. My own wife died in this war. I just do not follow the words as blindly as you do. They have been written and re-written so many times, how do we even know they are still the words Primis left us? How do we know that Primis even still exists? You heard what the queen said about him."

Danby laughed "The queen has her own agenda."

"What agenda does she have?" Ian asked looking for a rational answer

Danby shrugged "I cannot know her mind. Maybe she wishes to enslave us like she has her own people. Perhaps, she is jealous that some half breeds have power. Better yet, maybe she seeks our blood to retain her youth. Whatever the reason, she does not help us because of kindness. That is why when our war is over, I will not hesitate to take this planet from her by force."

"Do you really plan to wage war on her?" Ian asked stupefied

"She is one, we are many. This planet will belong to us soon enough." Danby replied with a gleam of madness in his eyes

"She has an army." Ian reminded him

"Do you really think her army will fight for a planet they have never even seen?" Danby asked

"If their queen orders it, yes." Ian said

"At first, they might, but no army is willing to die for something they do not believe in or even care about. Mark my words Ian, her army will abandon her and this planet will be ours." Danby reassured him

As the Twins stepped through the doorway onto Earth, they were impressed. She had combined many different things to create the planet. She had created a large land mass, surrounded by oceans. It was hot and dry her and her animals thrived. The enormous animals roamed in large herds, most eating from the plants and trees. They found Gaea bent over a giant egg, that was just beginning to hatch.

Gaea looked up at them and stood up. Caspian noted she did not look surprised to see either of them. She did not look bothered by the fact that had appeared, seemingly out of nowhere. As she stood up both of them were surprised height and appearance. She favored neither her mother or father. She was tall with a sturdy frame. She did not possess the frailty of the fae, who were known for their delicate, waif like appearance. Gaea looked like a woman who best any man in a wrestling match. Her face did not hold any of her mother's beauty or even her father's fine features. Her hair was the color of dirt, Caspian noted. Even tied back in a braid it had no shine or luster. She walked towards them both, but did not smile as she approached. In fact, it almost looked like a bull getting ready to charge them.

"Why are you here?" she demanded from them

"Allow me to introduce myself and my brother to you." Cree said in his most charming voice

"I know who you are and my question remains the same. Why are you here?" she asked gruffly

"I see our reputations proceed us!" Cree exclaimed happily

"Not in a good way." Gaea pointed out "I demand an answer to my question, which you must give." she reminded him

Cree's eyes narrowed at her for a moment. They were indeed bound by the Source to answer any question asked of them. Although, it had never been decreed the answer must be truthful. Cree had learned long ago that any rule given to him had gray areas.

"Your animals of course. They are the only of their kind in the universe, which makes them rare. We are the collectors of rare things." he answered formally letting her think she had bested him

Gaea eyed him suspiciously "You are also the collectors of souls. Sisue warned me about the two of you, since before I could even walk." she informed them

Cree opened his arms wide in defeat and shrugged "We have many jobs, that is true." he said sheepishly

Caspian looked around fascinated "What do you call this place?" he asked

Gaea was caught off guard by the question. She had

been told the bearded Twin rarely spoke. "This is Pangea." she answered

"It is odd for a planet to have only one land mass." he pointed out

"I took my inspiration from Lagoria. One land mass surrounded by oceans; it helps to keep my eco system intact." she told him

Caspian nodded at the idea. When he had created Lagoria, he had thought it would be better to keep everything contained in one spot. The oceans though had been an accident. He had been lonely that day and he was still a small boy, so he had wept in sorrow while thinking of all the people that would inhabit the planet. His tears had caused the great ocean to surround the Lagorians.

"Only one moon though?' he asked thinking of the six on Lagoria

"My moon does not house souls, so one is sufficient. Besides, the moons over Lagoria cause the sea there to be constantly churning. I need my sea creatures to have a more stable environment to flourish. Life cannot flourish amid chaos." she explained

"How true." Cree agreed wistfully

Gaea shot him a dirty look "What do you want?" she asked him rudely

"I have already answered that, we have come for an egg." Cree said losing patience with her tone

"What will you do with it? It cannot be introduced onto another planet; it would not survive." she told him

"We will give it to the Source of all life. He is like a giant child when it comes to new animals. He will be delighted to have one of these." Cree explained

Gaea knew she could not refuse the request, although she wanted to. She was bound just like them to the Source of all Life.

"You will take it and leave." she instructed them

Cree looked insulted at the demand "So soon? We haven't even looked around yet." he mocked her

"How did you get here? I did not invite you." she asked suspiciously

The Twins she knew were not allowed to go into any new planet or realm, unless they had been invited by its inhabitants. Once they had been somewhere though, they could enter freely with permission no longer needed. What no one ever realized when they heard this rule, was that they had already been everywhere. When the Source of all Life had thought this universe into existence, it was nothing more than cold lifeless orbs. The Twins had actually been the first thing brought into existence, nothing existed before them. Brought to life to help create the universe, in them was the building blocks of all life. It was Caspian who was directed to fill the planets with life. They never truly needed an invitation, because they had already been on every planet. The only thing that remained tricky for them was when a new realm was created. Earth was not a realm. Cree absolutely hated realms!

When the Source of all Life had found out what Caspian had done, he had given people their magical abilities. With magic they could create realms that were inaccessible to the Twins. A realm was a world, beside a world. A world that could not be seen by the naked eye, unless the creator of the realm allowed it to be seen. Already, six separate realms existed that they could not access. Not to mention that Cree was positive that something existed beyond the abyss, but even the Source could not access that.

"Long ago, before you terra formed this planet to create your animals, we were here." Cree finally explained "We would play here as children."

"You would play on a lifeless rock?" Gaea asked shocked

"We were brought into existence under an erupting volcano at the edge of the abyss. Lifeless rocks were a welcome change." Caspian confirmed to her

"Where were you brought to life?" Cree asked Gaea

"Do not try to charm me soul collector." Gaea warned him "I know you have the ability to look into my soul and know any answer you seek about me."

"You might be surprised to learn, that while we do have that ability, we rarely use it." Cree told her

"Why not?' she asked not really believing him

"To look into a soul and instantly know everything can become tedious. To see every life a soul has lived and every moment of those lives. To see things even they can't remember, is an occasional sport at best. It does not challenge the mind to know everything." Cree explained

"You expect me to believe that?" Gaea scoffed

Caspian braced himself, Cree could not tolerate being laughed at or mocked in any way. Caspian knew Gaea would pay a price for doing it.

Cree remained calm, although daggers shot out of his eyes at her "I don't care what you believe." he informed her "Our existence is endless, we must find our entertainment where we can. Now go and fetch our egg and we will leave this place." he ordered in a harsh tone

Even as powerful as Gaea knew she was, she knew she had

gone too far with him. She turned and walked to the nests she had been tending nearby. She picked up a football sized egg and returned to him.

She handed it to Cree and said "It was just laid this morning. It is a new species of dinosaur that I am introducing to the planet. It is the rarest among them all." she told him hoping it would placate him, Sisue had warned her what could happen if they became angry

Cree grabbed it and held it in his hands carelessly, twirling it around and throwing it up to catch it. Then he lifted it above his head and looked her straight in the eyes. As he smashed it into the ground, he brought a foot down hard stomping on it. The egg broke into pieces and a green liquid began oozing from it. He never once looked away from her as he destroyed the egg.

"Whoops." he said callously

Gaea's throat clenched in fear as she realized what danger she was in now. Sisue had warned her that Cree in particular was brutal and merciless when provoked into anger. She had only meant to stand her ground, not make him mad.

"Shall I get you another?' she stammered fearfully

A terrifying smile crossed Cree's face as he answered her "On second thought, I do not think your dinosaurs are as special as I thought. They do not look like they have the staying power a species needs to survive. In fact, I bet a single asteroid could wipe them all out." he told her and turned to Caspian "What do you think brother? Do you think a single asteroid would wipe them all out?" he asked seriously

Caspian felt the dread growing inside of him "I think it probably would." he answered

Cree looked back at Gaea now "Well we are sorry to have bothered you. If you will excuse us we have more important things to do." he said coldly

"I am truly sorry if I have offended you." Gaea said apologetically, knowing it was already to late

"Perhaps, the next time we meet, we will be shown more courtesy by you." Cree suggested and waved in their doorway

Gaea fell to her knees and wept after they had left. She looked around at the magnificent creatures that grazed peacefully nearby. She began to feel the ground rumble underneath her and watched as the dinosaurs all began running, sensing the danger. She looked up at the sky and saw a massive fireball hurtling towards them. She waved in her doorway and stepped through right before the impact. The impact wiped out every single dinosaur. It was then she learned that you did not go unpunished if you laughed at Cree.

CHAPTER 7

The humans had been on Fae for five days when the Twins returned. They had left for the caves hours ago, when the Twins began to climb the staircase. Amme awaited their arrival eagerly, hoping for news of her daughter.

She was bursting with anticipation as they greeted her and sat down, she could not remember the last time she had been this excited "Well, do you have news of Gaea?' she asked

"Better than that, we spoke to her." Cree exclaimed happily

Caspian pulled a photo from the inside pocket of his jacket and handed it to her. Amme did not see the lack of beauty that the Twins saw. Instead, she saw it through a mother's eyes.

"Do you see how she glows even now?" Amme gasped, immediately swelling with pride "She has her father's eyes I see." she whispered and ran her fingertip along Gaea's face

"She is spirited like you." Cree told her, but Amme failed to hear the irritation in his voice

Amme looked up "Is she? Tell me more of her." she begged

Cree spun a wonderful tale about Gaea. He made their interaction sound almost magical, but still believable enough for Amme. He left out the part where he destroyed everything, she had worked so hard on, or the fear he left in her.

"She is amazing Amme; you should be proud of the sacrifices you made for her." Cree finished

"Thank you for bringing this to me." Amme said truly grateful for the image of her daughter

"Well, it is not the only reason we have come." Cree admitted

"Oh?" Amme replied

"The humans will find the azurite they seek today." Cree informed her and she did not ask how he knew

"Then you should get down there! It seems our deal is almost complete." she said eager to get back to the picture she held

Cree and Caspian had stood to leave when Amme asked them almost in an afterthought "How does azurite complete their weapon? I have only ever known it to be a pretty stone, void of value unless in jewelry. A stone that can be found on any planet."

Cree turned back to her "Fae azurite is different my queen. I assure you the catalyst they need can only be found here." he reassured her

Amme shrugged accepting the answer. Too caught up in her own thoughts to give it any real thought. She saw Caspian's handkerchief had fallen from his pocket and was lying beside his chair. It must have fallen when he removed the picture for her.

"Caspian, you have left this." she called out to him picking it up

He hurried back over to retrieve it from her and as he did, he whispered a warning "You must keep your daughter away from him dark fae. Her life depends on it." then he turned and rejoined his brother as if nothing had been said

Amme did not let the smile fade from her face, until

they were gone. As she watched them walk across the meadow towards the caves, she finally let it drop.

Cree she decided always spoke in lies and half-truths. She knew azurite was a worthless stone, used only as decoration. He did however say the catalyst for their weapon could only be found here. So, she reasoned they must be secretly looking for something else. What though? She could think of nothing and decided to keep a much closer eye on the humans.

More importantly, why had Caspian warned her about Gaea's safety? Why was Cree a threat to her daughter? She knew Caspian would never give her the answer, but she knew someone who might have the answer.

She had kept an ear open for word about Sisue throughout the centuries. Sisue had never told her where she was taking Gaea or the other fae. Amme had assumed it was safer for all of them if she didn't know. A few centuries ago, she had heard of a powerful witch who lived in a golden temple, in another galaxy. Although it was another galaxy and it was said to be a witch, Amme knew it was Sisue. She had vowed to never seek either of them out, but if Gaea was in danger, she would break that vow. Amme waved in her doorway and hoped Sisue's energy on the other side would be enough to open it.

Amme was surprised when she stepped through, at the sight that greeted her. It felt like she had stepped into an oven, the heat was so intense. Sisue's golden pyramid lay in front of her, surrounded by sand. Amme looked around and saw nothing else. It went on for miles in every direction.

The fae had always been drawn to nature. They delighted in flowers, trees, grass and water. They loved the feel of the connection to the ethereal string that all living things had. Here in the dessert, it could be felt faintly at best. Amme knew she was no expert on the silver energy, but even she could still feel it.

It might not course through her body, the way the dark energy did, but it still existed in her. Why had Sisue chosen to raise Gaea in a place where it was so weak, she wondered.

"When you are done gawking around, come inside and join me. It is to hot outside for an old woman." Sisue called out to her from the doorway of the pyramid

Amme looked at Sisue, startled by her unexpected voice. She did not smile or wave in greeting, she simply began walking towards her.

When she reached the doorway, Sisue grabbed her by the shoulders and looked her up and down critically.

"Dark fae, you wear your pain like you wear your beauty." she said sadly

"And how is that?" Amme asked

Sisue let go of her shoulders and answered "For all to see." she said and turned "Come inside, we must have something very important to talk about, if you have finally sought me out."

Amme followed her inside and the door closed behind her. Inside the air was cool and refreshing. There in the middle of the pyramid stood the old fruit tree. Sisue reached up and plucked a pear from it and held it out to Amme. Amme shook her head, no at it. Sisue shrugged her shoulders and took a bite of it instead. She sat on the ground beneath the tree and waited for Amme to sit by her. Sisue finally swallowed and began to speak.

"Why have you come dark fae?' she asked

"I am concerned that Gaea is in danger." Amme told her

"Why?" Sisue asked

"Caspian warned me she was." Amme said

Sisue looked at Amme disappointed "So it was you that

sent the soul collectors to her. I wondered who had done it, but I never suspected you. I had thought you smarted then that Amme."

"You know of the Twins?" Amme asked surprised

"Of course, I do! My own daughter made a deal with them long ago. Tell me Amme what deal have you made with them?" Sisue asked

"Nothing really, I agreed to let the humans have azurite from Fae, in exchange for word of Gaea." Amme admitted embarrassed

"Why did you not just come to me for word of Gaea?" Sisue asked confused

"Because I promised you, I would not seek either of you out. I thought if the Twins could bring me news of her, no one would be the wiser. I thought no harm could come of it; the Twins are servants to life." Amme explained weakly

"Is that what they told you?" Sisue asked

"Is it not true?" Amme asked

"I suppose in a way it is. Do you understand what life is Amme?" Sisue asked

Amme looked confused by the question "I guess it is anything that is alive." she answered

"Life is pure chaos Amme. So many things in the universe can be explained and yet and equal amount cannot be explained. Sometimes it seems like the story of life is changing so constantly, it is hard to keep up with it. There is no rhyme or reason to any of it, it is pure chaos." Sisue told her

"I don't understand." Amme said

"Look at this tree Amme. Why do you think it grows every

type of fruit, when all others can only grow one kind of fruit?" Sisue asked

Amme shrugged "I assumed you created it that way."

"I do not have the power to create a tree. I have the power to help it grow and flourish, but I cannot create it. None of us can truly create anything. We can manipulate DNA and it seems like we are creating. Gaea can terra form a planet and it appears as if she created it. Without DNA though, we wouldn't be able to. DO you know who created DNA?" she asked

"No." Amme answered

"Neither do I! None of us do, it existed long before the first people. In each of the Twins are the building blocks of all life in existence and even they cannot truly create. A single teardrop from them would bring an ocean into existence, yet they would not be the ones who had created it. Once all trees grew like this one and then suddenly it changed, as if on a whim. No one can explain life, because it is nothing more than chaos. Life changes without explanation and it does not ask permission. The Twins serve this chaos Amme and they serve it well." Sisue explained

"Why would they want to hurt Gaea though if I have given them what they want?' Amme asked

Sisue shook her head at Amme "Because you haven't given them what they really want. They have requested it from you, but you did not listen. Cree is the one who always makes the offer, so the truth will be hidden somewhere in his words. Caspian only offers warnings, but they are always veiled. Neither of them will ever say directly to you what they want or warn about." Sisue counseled

"How am I supposed to know what they really want if they haven't told me?" Amme asked

"They have told you Amme, just not clearly. I suspect

whoever made the deal for the humans doesn't know what they agreed to either." Sisue told her

"That is easy enough to answer. Primis made the deal for the humans." Amme told her

"Primis is locked away in a Lagorian prison, he has been for centuries. The Lagorians discovered what he did." Sisue told her

"What did he do?' Amme asked

"He took genetic material from the moons above Lagoria and mixed it with the DNA to make the humans." Sisue told her

"The moons that house the souls? How is that even possible?" Amme asked shocked

"It seems Primis has a history of making deals with the Twins. They are the finders of rare things, if anyone could have gotten it, it was the Twins." Sisue answered

"How do I keep Gaea safe now?" Amme asked desperately

"It is not you who made Cree focus on Gaea. It was Gaea herself who provoked his wrath. She is stubborn and impetuous." Sisue said and then recounted the encounter Gaea had with the Twins

Amme sat in shock as she listened. This was nothing like the story Cree had told. Everything Gaea worked for had been destroyed in minutes and it was all her fault. If she had kept her promise to never look for Gaea, this never would have happened. The Twins would never have sought her out and she would still be safe. She had to figure out a way to keep her safe.

"She sounds like she has her father's temper." Amme finally said

"Paired with her mother's mouth!" Sisue exclaimed and Amme laughed

"Never a good combination." Amme agreed

"She knows who you are Amme. She knows of you and Alyks both. She knows the choice you made for her. I have never kept either of you a secret from her." Sisue told her kindly

"She does?" Amme gasped

"Of course, did you believe I wouldn't tell her?" Sisue asked

"I just assumed you would raise her as your own daughter." Amme admitted

"I did, but she knew where she came from. Gaea is a fae like me and there will only ever be one more besides us that will exist. She had the right to know who and where she came from." Sisue told her

"I saw the other like you, on the night my powers were sung in." Amme told her remembering her vision that night

"How do you know it was her?" Sisue asked curiously

"She glowed like you and Gaea do. Only she was so much brighter then either of you, it made your light look faint. She was tall like a giant and she fought against other giants. Above her a golden dragon rained down fire, to protect her. Their movements were synchronized, almost as if they were connected somehow. I do not know what she fought for, but I will never forget the words she spoke to me." Amme said recalling the scene

"What did she say?" Sisue asked

"She said, always protect your family." Amme told her "It is why I chose the dark energy. It was the only way to protect Gaea."

"So, you looked ahead in time, to see the fae who would save us all." Sisue said in awe

"Do you really think we will still be here when she is born?"

Amme asked

Sisue shook her head "No, only Gaea will still exist when that time comes, but our stories will shape her. Maybe, our souls will have the honor of meeting her someday, though." Amme stood up "I should go now, before the Twins notice I'm gone." she said

"Be wary of them dark fae." Sisue warned her

Amme looked at her and nodded I will, but I will also find a way to keep Gaea safe from them." she promised

After she had left a figure stepped out from behind the tree.

"Was that really her? She is so beautiful!" Gaea said

Sisue looked at her and nodded in agreement "Your mother has always been an extraordinary beauty, but she is also stubborn." Sisue told her

Gaea smiled down at the old woman "She seems fearless."

"That is exactly the problem. She will dive head first into anything if she believes the cause is justified." Sisue told her

"Do you think Cree will destroy her?" She asked worried

"Only if she allows him to." Sisue said

"Why would she allow him to destroy her?" Gaea asked shocked

"To save you." Sisue said, knowing Amme would keep her promise no matter what it took

CHAPTER 8

The humans had indeed found a large vein of azurite. They had come back to their encampment loudly and in great spirits. The end of the war was in their sights now. They stayed up late into the night drinking and singing. Tomorrow, Amme would go with them and remove it. Once it was mined and cleaned, they would finally go home. When they left, she could return to Thelry. Her deal with the Twins would be done and she could figure out how to keep Gaea safe.

The night had become quiet as she had contemplated her thoughts and Amme knew the sun would be rising soon. Amme noticed movement below and saw Ian sneaking around and trying to be quiet. He loaded his slung his pack over his shoulder and grabbed a shovel. When he started walking in the opposite direction of the caves, Amme grew suspicious. She knew the humans had come here for something besides azurite. If he thought he could sneak off into the and take it, he was wrong.

Ian walked deep into the trees until he found the one, he was looking for. It was taller than all of the others and the trunk would take the arms of six men to wrap around it. He dropped his backpack and began to dig at the base of it with his shovel. He had gotten less than a foot deep, when a voice interrupted the silence of the night.

"How dare you try to take anything from this planet that I did not give you." Amme said angrily

Ian turned around confused "What?" he asked

"What do you dig for human?" she roared

Ian looked down at the hole wondering how he could explain.

"Speak quickly or die slowly." she commanded

"I'm not trying to take anything! I am trying to leave something." he said frantically and reached inside of his pack

He pulled out a box and held it up for Amme to see "What is inside of it?" she asked suspiciously

He sat down hard and held it tightly against himself "My wife." he whispered

Amme understood immediately and felt a pang of regret "why did you bring her here?" she asked softening her tone

Ian stared off into the distance "She used to imagine this place to be beautiful. She thought it would be full of flowers and rivers, maybe evena few unicorns. It seemed almost magical to her." he said

"How did she die?" Amme asked thinking of Alyks now

"In the war. The very first day of the war to be exact. The building we lived in collapsed and killed her. I was trying to get home, but the streets were crowded with protestors. I couldn't get through to her, but I wonder everyday if I could have saved if I had." he explained

"If you had gotten through, you would also be dead." Amme told him knowing his fate would have been the same

Ian looked up at her now with tears in his eyes "I would have preferred that to living every day without her." he confessed

Amme understood exactly what he meant "It never gets easier. They say the pain dulls and life goes on, but it does not."

"Well, that's comforting." he said angrily

"I am not here to bring you comfort." she said "For ten thousand years I have waited for the pain of my loss to subside. Every day I wake up and for a brief moment, I forget he is gone. For a split second, before I open my eyes, I forget he is gone and that is the only reprieve I have known." she told him

"I know what you're talking about. That moment when you expect to open your eyes and see their face across from you." he said

Amme nodded "When you are almost sure you can hear them breathing, next to you and faintly smell them still." she said

"It never stops hurting?" he asked quietly

Amme closed her eyes and saw Alyks "It might for you, but he was the very air I breathed. Every day since he has been gone, I feel as if I'm suffocating." she answered

He held the box closer to him and let his tears flow unabashedly. He didn't know why he felt as if he could cry in front of her like this, but somehow, he knew she was safe. No one else around him felt safe to express his sorrow in this way, even his best friend Danby would not understand. She averted her eyes and let him weep.

She wondered how many loves he had lost each time his soul was re-born. She had only lost him one time and her heart had never healed. She couldn't fathom the countless losses all souls must endure. The un-ending heartbreak, life after life.

"Come I know the perfect place for her." Amme said when his tears had finally exhausted themselves

Ian stood up silently and followed Amme through the dense forest. They came out of the trees into a clearing filled hyacinth. The smell over powered the air and reminded Ian of his wife instantly. Amme took the box from him and gently placed it among tiny flowers that had just begun to bloom.

She reached out for the silver string and the dark energy stepped aside. Slowly at first, because she was unused to manipulating the ethereal energy. She began to grow the plant up around the box. The flowers grew tall and absorbed the box into their roots. Just as the plant reached its full height, the first rays of the sun reached out and touched the plant with its warmth. Ian was mesmerized as the light shown down on the spot where his wife now rested.

"It's perfect, thank you." he whispered to Amme so as not to break the spell

Amme was surprised to feel a tear slide down her cheek and wiped it away quickly "She will be in good company here; my own husband lies next to her." she said and pointed at Alyks's own resting spot.

"I hope to see her again, if you and fate will allow it." he told her

"Fate?' she asked

"The war." he reminded her "The war will decide my fate."

Amme straightened herself "We should go then and retrieve your stone, so you may be reunited with your wife again."

"One more minute, please." he asked staring at the spot where his wife was

Amme looked to where Alyks was "Yes, one more minute can be spared." she agreed

As they finally made their way back to the encampment the sun was high and Danby was furious.

"Where have you been?" he yelled angrily at Ian

Ian looked at him sheepishly. How could he explain that he and the Queen of Thelry had lost all time staring at their dead spouses' gravesites? Each lost in their own memories, they had stood together in silence for hours. The silence healing a void in each of them.

"In the woods." Ian finally stammered in embarrassment

"In the woods!" Danby screamed in disbelief "In the woods! He shouted again and grabbed the table next to him and flipped it over furiously "We fight a war and you are galivanting in the woods?"

The dark energy which had been dormant in Amme, rose up at his anger. It wanted to reach out and see what he held in his true heart, but Amme held it back. She knew the dark energy would only find madness.

"I'm sorry, but I had my own business to attend to. I lost track of time." Ian explained embarrassed that Danby was causing a scene

Danby looked Amme up and down in disgust "The two of you had personal business?' he asked lewdly

Ian took his meaning clearly "Do not disparage the Queen who has generously given us what we need. I had something to take care of and now my business is finished. Let us get on with our day." he said through clenched teeth, outraged by the insinuation

The group of men around them began to gather up their supplies, eager for the confrontation to be over. Danby stared at Ian for a moment, trying to decide if he was going to let the matter drop. Finally, he turned and righted the table. Ian sighed in relief, Danby was his oldest and closest friend. He did not ever want to fight with him. In only a few minutes the team was ready and Amme let them lead the way. She would remove the azurite herself; she did not want them destroying the cave for a few stones.

She noticed as they walked, Danby had slowed his pace and soon was walking beside her. She did not care for this human at all. He was quick to anger and she felt it burning inside of him non-stop. It lay just beneath the surface of the facade, he presented to everyone around him. He seemed charming and good natured, quick to smile and presented himself as a defender of the weak. Yet, Amme could see it was all a clever mask he hid behind. Danby reminded her of the Emperor, only mimicking true emotion. She knew inside of Danby was a darkness, only men seemed to possess. A Darkness that craved the pain and suffering of others. His trued heart wanted violence and the only happiness he had ever experienced was when he was inflicting pain on others. When he was near her, her own darkness begged her to be set free on him. She fought to contain it, lest she lose control and unleash his own darkness upon him. She knew it would consume him as he begged her for mercy.

"Did you finally feel what a human man felt like?" he asked her lewdly

Amme did not let his foul suggestion rattle her, she simply looked at him calmly "If you ever speak to me like that again, I will remove your tongue from your mouth. I have no use for any human and I will remind you that you have not secured what you have come here for yet. If you hope to leave this planet with it, you will heed my warning, human." she explained

"You don't scare me." Danby informed her boldly

Amme smiled coldly at him "Then you are truly a fool. Your nightmares are child's play compared to what I will do to you. Do not underestimate my power human, it will most likely be the death of you." she said and walked ahead of him

CHAPTER 9

The Twins entered the cell where Primis was being detained. Cree chuckled at the idea of calling it a cell. Lagorians did not ever break their own laws, so no prison had ever been built here. The Lagorians were a very serious people, who took their duty to be almost sacred. Primis was the first among them to even be convicted of a crime. The planet had been in turmoil on what to do. Finally, they have voted collectively that the oldest thirteen among them would decide his fate. He had been imprisoned indefinitely here; a suite of rooms had been cleared to become his cell. He was not allowed to leave, but he was allowed to have visitors. It was a well-furnished suite of rooms, equipped with anything he needed to continue his research. For all of his luxuries and freedom he looked up at them devastated when they walked through the door.

"Why such the long face? I thought you would be happier to see us!" Cree greeted him jovially

Primis tried to smile weakly "I am imprisoned here, while my humans fight another war." he reminded Cree

"You hardly suffer here." Caspian told him sickened by his despair

"I do suffer though!" Primis protested "The humans once again destroy everything I built for them. Instead of being there to guide them, I am being punished for creating them."

"Good thing we are here then!" Cree exclaimed delighted at Primis's misery "The promise I made to you is almost complete.

The humans will have everything they need to complete their weapon. The war will soon be over, old friend."

Primis shook his head, as the Twins seated themselves "I still do not understand how azurite will help them. It is a useless stone, explain to me how it will make their weapon work."

"I would have thought you would trust me by now. Have I ever not fulfilled a promise I made to you?" Cree asked dodging the question

Primis stared at the man and thought of his dealings with him. Many times, he asked for the Twins help and every time he got exactly what he had asked for. Even with their help though, it always seems to end in disaster. He had gone to them begging for the genetic code from the heavens. The place where all souls rested until they were ready to be dropped onto Lagoria. The Lagorians were tasked long ago to be the soul keepers, until they were ready to take form. Primis had always wondered what a race of people, made from the purest form of the soul would be capable of. He was convinced they would extraordinary like the Titans had once been. Capable of finding their way back to the Source of all Life. He had built an entire civilization for the humans and given strict laws to live by. Laws that would ensure their success. He had treated the first generation, like they were his own children. He had secured a planet on the edge of the universe, where they would be safe. He had educated them in the sciences and technologies they would need for survival. Soon though they began to crave power, in a way he had never seen before. They always wanted more then he gave them. More than they needed! He watched as they began to take from one another. If he gave them each an apple, they immediately began to fight. They would fight until someone had all of the apples. Then the person with all of the apples, wielded their power over the others. It did not matter what it was, they fought over everything. They would rather fight then to simply share. Primis quickly learned power was the only resource they cared about.

The problem with that, was power looked different to each of them. While one of them thought the food supply was the key to power, another believed it was the water. Another would think the land itself was the key to power. Soon they developed a currency system to barter with one another for power. The person who gre the apples, must pay the other person for the water. The person with the water had to pay the person who controlled the land. The person who controlled the land had to pay the person for the apple to eat. It became an unending mindless circle. Primis grew frustrated over the mindless fighting, because all of the others who had nothing would fight to take something for themselves. The entire race soon adopted the motto, if it is not given, it is taken. The humans lived and gladly died by this creed. Primis came to a place where he could no longer control them. Then the Lagorians discovered what he had done and punished him for it. Punished and given an ultimatum, if he could not think of a way to get control of the humans he would be sent to the heavens. Lagorians did not return from the heavens for re-birth, they were instead absorbed into the moons. He was becoming desperate, trying to think of a solution. Hopefully, Cree had bought him some more time to solve his problem.

"No, you have always fulfilled every promise you made." Primis relented

"Then trust that is what we will do now." Cree reassured him

Caspian stared at Primis in pure disbelief. How could he not realize by now, that every deal he made with Cree ended this way for him? No one was safe from Cree and almost everyone bought into his fake persona. Even queen Amme had made a deal with him. Caspian was certain she knew Ian housed her dead husband's soul and still she kept up her end of the deal. Even if she did eventually find out what Cree had actually done to Gaea, there was nothing she could do about it. No one could stop Cree, except of course the Source of all Life and he didn't seem to care what Cree did.

"I still don't understand how you got queen Amme to agree to help the humans, that fight to kill magic. I would think a fae, especially a dark one would refuse?" Primis mused

"She doesn't know." Cree revealed

"What if she finds out?" Primis gasped imagining her fury

"It won't matter, she will remain loyal to her husband's soul. She does not understand, but even now she protects him. By the time she finds out, it will be too late." Cree told him

"To late for what?" Primis asked confused

"To late to stop the fate that awaits them all. Their story was written long ago, they just don't know it yet." Cree said and looked out the window at the waves crashing into the glass soundlessly. The violence of the ocean had always pleased him. It was the purest form of chaos and he often wondered how anyone could find it peaceful. He had seen entire continents be swallowed by it. The ocean had no emotion, just raw power that left destruction in its wake.

"She is a dangerous one to trick." Primis warned, not understanding the power of the Twins completely

Caspian chuckled softly at the warning. Cree was the most dangerous being in the universe and no one ever realized it, until it was too late. Caspian had always found it strange that the two of them could just appear out of nowhere and no one questioned them about their origin. Their presence was always just accepted as normal.

"There are a few more dangerous than her." Caspian

pointed out to him

Primis shot him a terrified look "She is a destroyer of worlds! There is nothing more dangerous than that."

Cree sat back and crossed his legs "She only destroyed one world." he said and held up a single finger to Primis

"One is plenty." Primis responded outraged "What if she sets her sights on the humans, when she discovers the truth? What is to stop her from destroying Huma?" he asked

Cree shrugged his shoulders, un-bothered at the idea "If she destroys the humans, I guess you will just have to make more."

"Make more! I am not baking cookies, being gobbled up by greedy children. I cannot simply make more." he replied outraged at the simplistic suggestion of his work

Cree laughed at him "That is exactly what you're doing, you fool. You have combined ingredients to create a new species. No one asked you to do it, you simply decided it was a good idea. You reasoned if you had the ability, it gave you the right. You grew tired of being a caretaker to the souls. You grew so weary of it, you decided to try your hand at being a creator. You play at being a God and comfort yourself with denial. The humans could be destroyed a thousand times and you would always make more. That is why your own people punish you Primis, they see the full scope of your madness." he answered cruelly

Primis was shocked by Cree's words. Never had Cree anything but helpful and friendly. It was like a mask had suddenly slid down to reveal a darker side to him.

"I thought you were my friend." Primis replied

Cree leaned forward in his chair closer to Primis and stared at him coldly "Did you believe that because I was kind to you or was it because I gave you what you wanted?" he asked

"I have always wondered the same thing." Caspian chimed in "Do you think friendship stems from kindness or deeds?" he asked Primis

"Are you both mad?" Primis asked them shocked

The Twins glanced at one another for a moment and then answered in unison "Probably."

Primis stood up angrily and shouted at them both "If anything happens to the humans, I will never forgive either of you!"

Cree and Caspian stood simultaneously and straightened their jackets and ties. They turned to leave, but Cree stopped in the doorway before leaving.

"I do not seek your forgiveness, but you will seek me out again. If I were you, I would remember to hold my tongue in the future. A steep price must always be paid for speaking to me that way." he said and Primis stood speechless as the door shut behind him

The table at the camp was filled with large chunks of azurite. Even in the bright sunlight, everyone could see they glowed from within.

"I have never seen azurite glow this way before." Danby said mesmerized by the sight

"It explains why Cree said we had to get it from here." Ian replied

"It has an energy source inside of it. I have to run some tests, but it looks like this will power our weapon." their science officer told them

"You did not bring the weapon to my planet, did you?" Amme asked

Ian shook his head "No, we only brought the detonator to make sure it could be powered." he reassured her

"We could bring some for you, if you ask really nice." Danby told her trying to gauge her reaction

Amme looked at him expressionlessly "Do you realize how easily I could kill you?" she asked him

"I don't think it would be as easy as you think." Danby replied and winked

"That is exactly what makes your kind so stupid. Your confidence hides your weakness from you. I could snap my fingers and you would fall down dead. You wouldn't even realize your own stupidity until right before your final breath. Your entire species is like a colony of insects." she informed him

Danby started to take a step forward in anger and Ian out a hand on his shoulder to stop him "Easy buddy, we're almost finished here." he reminded him quietly

"Two more days and you leave this planet." Amme reminded them all and walked away

When she was out of sight, Danby exploded in rage "Why do I hate her so much!" he exclaimed and began knocking things over

"Come on Danby!" Ian yelled "We're almost done here, contain it for a couple more days." he said trying to reason with him

Danby turned his fury on Ian now "Would you stop defending her all of the time! Have you suddenly given up on everything you believe in or are you falling in love with a witch?" he yelled back angrily

Ian's face flushed in anger now "Of course not!" he yelled

back

"I'm not so sure man." Danby accused "I see the way you look at her. It wouldn't be your fault, she probably put a spell on you." he said egging him on

"Shut your mouth." Ian warned

Danby got closer to him, until their noses were almost touching "I wouldn't be surprised if she has you bathing in blood in the moonlight soon." he said

Ian shoved him back hard "I said shut your mouth, Danby." he warned

"You want to fight me to defend your witch?" Danby asked shocked "I am the one who helped you pull out your dead wife, from underneath that wall! I carried her from the rubble for you. She died because of people like that witch and now you defend them?" Danby asked outraged

Ian felt his own anger deflate at the mention of his wife "Of course not!" he said and felt his shoulders sag

Danby saw his friend's distress and clapped him on the shoulder "We're almost done! Soon you will be home and never have to see this place again." he told him

All Ian could think about though, was that he was leaving his wife behind.

CHAPTER 10

Amme watched the Twins as they inspected the azurite. The humans were explaining to them in great detail how it had powered their detonators. The Twins feigned interest, but Amme could see they looked bored. She sat down on her throne and awaited their arrival on the rooftop.

As the Twins slowly walked up the stairs, Caspian remarked "This can't be all Cree, this deal seems to tame for you. I would have expected more damage." he said thinking the destruction on earth would not be enough to satisfy Cree

Cree laughed softly at the question "You know me too well, brother. I have a secret, but you must wait like all of the others to find out what it is." he teased

"At least provide a hint." Caspian coaxed knowing Cree loved to brag

Cree thought long and hard before finally saying "We shall be visiting Thelry soon."

Caspian did not let his shock show "We haven't been there since it first began crawling with new life. I will be curious to see the changes." he remarked and Cree smirked in response

Caspian knew Cree would sometimes disappear for days at a time, by himself. Anytime Caspian would go home to take care of the changelings, Cree would usually disappear. Caspian hated the heat and the stench of their home at the edge of the abyss, but he hated Cree even more. He knew that Cree was making deals with people when he disappeared like that, but his absence was always welcome.

Caspian let his mind wander back to the time, before Cree had existed. When the Source of all Life had called himself Soren and the Timekeeper had tried to love them both. Sora, the Timekeeper had tried to find the good in Soren, but had failed. Soren was impossible to love, he was impetuous and cruel. He demanded everything to be exactly how he wanted it and if you failed to please him his punishments were severe.

Sora began to argue with Soren and he could not destroy Sora, as much as he wanted to. Every Source was given one billion years to tell their story with all the souls. They could create the universe in any way they desired, but every Source must have a Timekeeper. Time and Creation had to exist in pairs. When a new Source was awoken to tell a new story, a new Timekeeper reset time for them both. It had been this way since the souls had begun to long for more and it could not be changed.

Caspian hated this story though and always dreaded when it was Soren's time to awaken again. He did have the advantage of remembering though, Cree could not. Cree did not know he only existed in this story, none of the others told the same story. Caspian was infinite, Cree was not. Each time Cree was created, he believed it was the first time. Caspian knew exactly how this story would play out; it always ended the same. This time though he had noticed small differences, almost imperceptible to anyone who had not seen it before. They were just little changes, but he was curious as to what it meant. He knew Soren was up to something, but couldn't figure out what. Although it could mean absolutely nothing, because the Source after all was only a child. A child who had been trapped inside of a man's body so he could not be found. Hidden away, as punishment to his parent's souls for wanting to tell their own story. For wanting nothing more than to feel the connection of another soul to their own.

"What are you thinking about?" Cree asked irritably unable to access Caspian's thoughts

"Home." Caspian replied knowing Cree could not connect with any of thoughts that had existed before Cree's creation

It made Cree so angry when he could not see his brother's thoughts. He could never understand how Caspian could mask his thoughts from him. What Cree had never realized was that he himself wasn't real, but merely a wish Caspian had made one day as a boy. When Caspian had been abandoned by Soren and Sora had been confined to the paper realm, he had grown lonely. The lonely little boy had made a wish for a companion and Cree had appeared in his shadow one day. Slowly, he had made his way out of the shadow. This was all Cree could remember, he could not fathom that time had existed before him. He could never have imagined that Caspian existed infinitely in every Source's storyline, not just Soren's. Cree did not understand that Caspian's energy always had existed, even without him. Cree only knew this story, because this was the only one, he existed in.

"Stop thinking of home!" Cree demanded angrily

"Why does it bother you when I think of home?" Caspian asked innocently, although he knew the answer

"You know why." Cree said angrily

"I was born first; you cannot be angry with that." Caspian pointed out, enjoying Cree's frustration

"You do not need to think of a time before I existed. Nothing mattered in your life before me brother." Cree demanded of him

"You would not be here if that were true." Caspian

answered

"No truer words have ever been spoken!" Cree said angrily "I sometimes think you forget why I am here. You forget how it was I first found you Caspian. A frail, lonely boy......so desperately lonely. Sitting on a rock as the lava flowed all around you, knowing only your misery kept you company. The air to thick to breathe, as the lava spit up and burned you, crying to yourself. I saved you from that fate Caspian, don't ever forget that." he reminded him

"Saved me? You tricked me!" Caspian said growing angry at the version of the story Cree loved to tell

Cree shrugged his shoulders, unconcerned by that little detail "You made a deal with me Caspian. You should not have made it without thinking of the consequences first. Why do think everyone is so quick to strike a deal with me Caspian? They only think of what they want and cannot see how it might affect them. You wanted a companion so badly; you didn't care how you got one. Not just a companion though! You wanted a brother. You didn't care how you got one, you never stopped to ask yourself if you would like me. You just agreed without thought." Cree told him

Caspian sighed heavily in frustration. He could not tell Cree that this had happened many times already. That even as he sat drying desperately as a boy, he was powerless to stop it, because it wasn't his story. He could not tell Cree the truth of their origins, because even if he tried nothing would come out of his mouth. Caspian was truly a servant to life and he could not alter the course of the storyline given to him. He had not sprung from the primordial ooze; he was the primordial ooze embodied. Everything must exist in pairs, that was true, but this Source made them walk side by side, instead of together. This Source broke up the pairs for reasons Caspian could never understand.

"You're doing it again." Cree told him in frustration

"We must go home after this; I need to check on the changelings." Caspian told him

"You may go home after this alone; I will be going to Thelry." Cree informed him

Caspian simply nodded; he had already seen the outcome of this many times.

Amme waited patiently for the Twins to settle in before she spoke. She noticed Caspian looked uncomfortable and wondered what was wrong with him.

"Are you well, Caspian?" She asked

"I am fine queen Amme. My brother and I were just discussing old memories." he replied

Amme eyed him so suspiciously "I am surprised that two beings like yourselves, dwell on something so mundane as the past."

Cree cleared his throat "What type of beings do you perceive us to be?' he asked curiously

"I cannot say what you are, but I know you are very old and unlike anything I have ever seen before." she told him truthfully

"I'm sure the universe is full of things you have never seen before." Caspian said calmly

Amme let her gaze linger on him a moment "I'm sure that is true, but I have a feeling the two of you are entirely unique." she said

"You make us blush with your assumptions." Cree said flirting

Amme looked at him now "I doubt you have ever blushed before." she informed him

Cree threw his hands in the air as if flabbergasted "We are neither special, nor unique. Just two servants of life who must wander the universe to fulfill our duties." he explained

Amme smirked at his lies, thinking about what he had done to Gaea "Why are you here? Our deal is concluded, the humans have what they need and I have seen Gaea. Those were our terms and they have been met." she reminded them both

Cree slapped his knee jovially "Quite right! We are only here to ensure the humans leave this place untouched, as promised."

"They load their ships even as we speak." Caspian reassured her

Amme peeked over the edge of the tower and saw indeed; they were loading their ships.

"Will you miss them?" Cree asked sarcastically

Amme held her temper at the question. Cree had thought himself so clever bringing Alyks's soul here. She supposed, he thought he could manipulate her with Ian. What he did not understand was that Amme had strong beliefs on that matter. The darkness had long ago shared with her the secret knowledge of souls. They are only meant to live a life once. A soul may have many different lives, but each is unique. To live a life over and over again would only pollute the soul with the pain left behind. Amme knew she could have awoken Alyks's soul a thousand times already, but at what cost to him? To know he would face his own death time after time. A soul believed it only lived once, if it was given the knowledge of its own creation, all of their stories would change. Fate itself, would no longer control the outcome of their lives. Instead, a soul would seek out its old life and no soul would ever rest peacefully. His soul would have become corrupted by the torment of it all.

"No, I will not miss them." she replied "I will not miss any of them."

Cree stood up abruptly "Well then, our business is concluded and we shall say farewell." he announced

"Farewell." Amme said politely

"Will you join us to say goodbye to the humans?" Caspian asked

"No." Amme said

"Very well." Cree said and held out his hand to Amme

Amme shook it quickly, shuddering at his touch. Then Caspian held out his hand to her. Amme took it and as their hands touched an image flashed in her mind. It was an image of Cree walking towards her palace in Thelry. Amme locked eyes with Caspian and knew he had shown it to her. Cree would seek her out again and she must be ready.

CHAPTER 11

As Ian landed the ship on Huma, he felt a pang of regret. He had not got the chance to say goodbye to queen Amme. He felt in debt to her for the kindness she had shown him, when he buried his wife. He knew in his heart, no matter the outcome of the war, her resting place would remain undisturbed.

"It's good to be home." Danby said to them as they landed

"It is, isn't it?" Ian agreed

"Tomorrow we will end the war and have our planet back." Danby said

Ian looked around at the ruined buildings and rubble everywhere "What's left of it anyway."

"We will rebuild and with the resources from Fae we will be stronger than ever." Danby told him

"Unless we start another war that way, then we will only be weaker." Ian reminded him

Danby laughed "One witch is hardly a war! Fae does possess an army only a queen."

"A very powerful queen. A queen that rules over every planet in the universe." Ian said

"Even a powerful queen is no match for our army. You worry too much Ian." Danby reprimanded him and unbuckled himself as the doors of the ship opened

"You do not worry enough, Danby." Ian said to the empty

seat beside him

Miori walked through the makeshift camp, towards her own tent. She had just checked on the wounded and spoken with the healers. They had the advantage in this war, since some of their magical abilities included healing. They may be called half breeds, but Miori knew they were superior to the humans. Even if they had been treated like slaves.

Miori had been raised in the camps where all half breed children and their parents were forced to live. Given only menial jobs and not allowed to attend school. She had been born into a society that had lost all hope and had long ago accepted their own fate. They had allowed their children to be sterilized when they turned eighteen and accepted all law without question. Miori knew the universe was filled with magic, but the people of Huma feared it. To them magic was like an unknown disease that must be eradicated. When the first children were born, that had been fathered by men of different planets, no one could have predicted this outcome. No matter what they did though, the humans could not magic from infecting their bloodlines.

Miori was grateful for the mother she had been born to. Her mother refused to let her spirit be broken. She had met Miori's father when she was an ambassador to Cala. She had returned to Huma unaware she was pregnant, or she never would have come back. She was sent to the camps as soon as it was discovered she was pregnant. She had regaled Miori with bedtime stories of her handsome father. He was a government official in Cala and sat high in the king's court. She taught Miori and the other children how to read and do math. She always encouraged Miori to use her magic, so it could grow stronger. She had taught Miori to embrace her magic and not fear it. She only forbids it's use when the soldiers would come.

Sometimes the soldiers would get drunk and come to the camp late at night. Those with the gift of sight would know when it was coming and the oldest in the camp would take the children away. The rest would stay behind and pay the price the soldiers demanded. Growing up Miori had not understood what happened on those nights. When she returned in the morning with the other children, she would only see the destruction. The screams from the people at the camp could be heard from where the children were hidden, but they never knew what caused them. The whole camp would be torn apart, the people would be bloodied and bruised, but no one ever spoke of it. She had not fully understood the horror inflicted upon them until she had turned seventeen.

The warning had come to them from a woman with the gift of sight. The children were being prepared to leave and Miori was begging her mother to let her stay.

"Please mother, I can protect you!" she had pleaded

"Next year, when you are eighteen you must stay. Until then Miori, you must go with the others." her mother had refused

Miori had finally relented, but had snuck away from the other children when they had gone to sleep. For a few miles she had walked back towards camp. In the silence of the night, she could hear the screams of her people. She was determined she would help her mother though and did not let her fear stop her.

When she finally saw the camp in the distance she was shocked at the sight. The soldiers were in a frenzy destroying everything around them. The men were being beaten, while the women were being dragged away to be assaulted in a very different way.

That is when she saw her mother being dragged by her hair, across the ground as a soldier screamed at her "Stop fighting, you filthy magic lover. I will show you tonight what real men do."

Miori could see he seemed so angry and yet he was enjoying the way his anger felt. He felt powerful and something deeply broken inside of him thought it felt good. Something inside of Miori broke free in that moment and the wind began to rage around her. She felt everything become alive with electricity and she knew it obeyed her. The soldiers began to panic as everything around them began to blow away with the force of the wind. Soon they began to run, thinking a tornado was upon them. Miori began to walk towards the camp and the closer she got the harder the wind blew. The soldier holding her mother by the hair was the last to give up and leave. He looked up, before he let go of her mother and his face was burned into her brain. Miori knew in that moment if she ever saw him again, she would kill him.

Miori rushed to her mother and the wind suddenly stopped. Her mother looked up at her terrified and Miori fell to the ground to hold her.

"Why do they do this?" Miori asked confused

Her mother clung to her and cried "Because that is the way of men." she replied through her tears

"Surely, not all men do this?" Miori asked desperately

"Not all, but enough that you can never feel safe." her mother told her sadly

It was the next morning that Miori gathered the people of the camp together. She vowed to them that a change must be made and she was going to lead the way to change. The future of their people depended on that change, she warned them all. Enough of the people agreed, mostly the younger among them. The older generations had already lived with this way of life, so long they knew nothing else. This is when the protests began. The protests were meant to show the people of the city that they were peaceful and meant no harm with their magic. Miori felt as if they were making headway, until the final day in the city. The day when the soldier hit the old man in the face with his gun. When he had turned to look at Miori, she had recognized his face. He was the soldier who had been dragging her mother, across the dirt. The wave of anger that had shot from Miori in that instant had leveled the city. She had never looked back on that day with remorse or regret. If war and violence was what men desired, she would give it to them. All of the half breeds had joined the cause then and used their magic to drive the soldiers back. Now they occupied what was left of the cities all over the planet. While those without magic hid and fought in the cover of night.

Miori reached her own tent and sighed in relief at the sight of it. She wanted to be alone and think. She had heard the whispers of her spies about a new weapon being built. As she stepped inside though, her heart sank at the sight of who waited for her.

"I thought I made it very clear I was not interested." she told the man as she walked across the floor and snatched a book from his hand, he had been thumbing through

Cree smiled broadly at her "Living in the camps has left you ill-mannered I see." he said pleasantly

"A proper greeting is a sign of good breeding." Caspian said from the chair he was sitting in

"Well, I find it rude to find the two of you in here uninvited and pilfering through my things." she informed them both coldly

Cree clasped his hands behind his neck and contemplated her words "I have never understood that all souls have to collect things. Do none of you realize that when you die, all of your trinkets become a burden to someone else?" he asked seriously deciding to ignore her statement

"I think they do it because it makes their lives seem more real to them." Caspian weighed in

Miori laughed at them both "We do it because every time we want to eat, we do not want to go in search of a fork or a pan. If I want to read a book, I want to have one available. If I need to write something down, I do not need to go in search of a pen or paper. We collect these things to make our lives easier." she explained

Both of them thought about her explanation and found it to be reasonable. Each of them gave her a slight nod of acceptance.

"This is the last offer I will make to you and your people. The planet Fae, will soon be under my control. Take your people and flee there before it is too late. You will be free to create a world where magic is accepted." Cree told her

"I thought Thelry controlled the planet, Fae?" Miori asked intrigued

"They do, but in a few days, it will belong to me." Cree said offering no further explanation

"Why would we leave Huma? This is our home; this is what we fight for." Miori told him

"Aren't you tired of war?' Cree asked

"Yes, but we will win soon. I won't leave Huma like I have been defeated and let the humans rise up again. Our fight is a just one." she told him

"Believe me when I say, every war ever fought was because of a just cause. The bodies of the dead could be piled up and reach the heavens because of just causes." Caspian said wisely

"Never the less, we will stay and fight." Miori replied "Why do you keep coming to me with offers?" she asked them both

"Only to save you. I have already explained we are servants to life." Cree replied humbly

"Yet, no matter how often you say it, I never believe you. There is something about the two of you I do not trust." Miori informed them

Cree shook his head sadly "What more can I do to convince you? The offer stands for two more days, after that it will be too late."

"What do you mean too late?" Miori asked suspiciously

Caspian stood up "He means your war will be over." he said and started to leave the tent

"How can you know that?" Miori asked "Even those with the gift of sight cannot see anything two days from now." she asked

Cree shrugged in response and followed Caspian "All wars must end Miori. History is written by those who survive it." he turned to her just before he stepped out and said "If you change your mind simply call my name and I will hear you."

CHAPTER 12

Amme listened quietly as Fredrick gave her a report on everything that had happened in her absence. He did not favor Alyks in looks, but he had the same temperament.

"You were gone longer than usual this time grandmother." he said when he had finally concluded his report

Amme's face gave no expression when she answered "Unforeseen circumstances kept me detained." she answered vaguely

"I don't know how a planet void of people could have offered unforeseen circumstances." he remarked

Amme smiled at him "You remind me so much of your grandfather." she told him

Fredrick chuckled at this "I have seen his portrait every day of my life and I must say I disagree."

Amme looked at the old man sitting across from her "Your grandfather was quiet like you. Always listening and plotting his next move, almost as if life were a chess game. Asking questions that could seem so meaningless, that you did not understand the true purpose of them." she said

"What was their true purpose?" Frederick prompted

"Information, of course. You ask the same kind of questions Frederick. Tell me, do you play chess with life?" she asked curiously, realizing she had never really gotten to know him

"It would be impossible to play chess with the life I have been given." he told her

"Why?' she asked

"I was born into a kingdom of an immortal queen. There is no real place for the princes of the kingdom here. We are not taught to be rulers, because we will never become rulers. We are at best, a sad collection of dolls displayed for the people to see. Even our births have become meaningless. I could try and manipulate the outcome, but it will never change." he told her

"The birth of a prince is a grand celebration." she reminded him

Frederick looked at her now seriously "Do you even remember the name of the newest prince, born less than a month ago?" he asked her

"Of course, I do! His name is............." Amme stared off into to the distance trying to remember and becoming frustrated "It is on the tip of my tongue."

Frederick sat back and said gently "No matter, it is not the first name you do not remember."

"I am very busy with my duties, as you well know Frederick." she admonished him

"It is more than that though, isn't it? We are your descendants, but we age as you remain the same. I can't imagine the pain you must have felt as you watched your own sons grow old and die. Then you repeated it with their sons. It must be a heavy weight indeed to outlive all of those you love." he consoled her

"I love all of you." she told him half heartedly

Frederick shook his head "No you don't and no one can

blame you for that. Your never-ending youth, brings with it perpetual loss. Even an immortal queen must close off her heart eventually."

"So, what would you have me do?' she asked shocked to hear his truth

"There is nothing you can do grandmother. You cannot change your own fate." he answered

"Well then I will tell you a secret, I have learned in my many years." she offered

"What is it?" he asked amused

"Life has a way of surprising you. Just when you think it has nothing more to show you, something will come along you don't expect." she said

Frederick sighed heavily at the thought "I'm counting on it grandmother. I could use something unexpected." he confessed

Amme was alone in her room, thinking about Frederick's words. As she looked into the mirror, she saw the same face she always did. She had not aged a day since Sisue had sung in her power. Alyks had used to joke with her when he began to age, that he was robbing the cradle. It did not matter that they were the same age, she was forever young.

Frederick was right of course, no matter how much she denied it. She had stopped taking an interest in her heirs long ago. Males were only ever born to their bloodline and she often wondered if her heart would have been moved if a girl had been born. It was doubtful, but maybe.

Generations of princes had been raised in the palace. Some more vocal with their dissatisfaction then others. Some were even bitter towards their fate rather than grateful. Some of them used the freedom their title and rank afforded them, truly understanding the advantages. These few knew since the crown would never be their responsibility, they had freedom. They could pursue their passions, some becoming master painters, architects and scholars. Others had used the freedom to travel the universe and explore, seeking adventure. They had all been given a life to do as they wished. She might not give them the love they sought, but she took care of them all.

She took one last look at herself and made a vow to herself to get to know them better. She would try harder for their sakes.

Danby slammed his hand down on the table in anger "Do you think she did something to it?" he bellowed at everyone in the room

The science officer shrugged, not having any real explanation for what had happened to the azurite "The stones still glowed when we unloaded them. I don't know how she could have sabotaged the azurite after we left, but anything is possible."

They all stared down at the azurite on the table. The glow that had powered the stones was gone. They could no longer power the detonators of their weapon.

"Perhaps, it is time to consider peace talks." Ian finally said defeated

"Are you mad?" Danby asked him outraged at the suggestion

"What other choice do we have? Without our weapon we cannot win the war. The half breeds have driven us from every city. What few soldiers we have left cannot fight much longer. Our supplies are depleted and we will lose, if we don't find a solution." Ian pointed out

"When did you become so weak?" Danby asked in contempt

"I am not being weak, only rational." Ian said angrily

"Were you being rational the day we voted you the general of this army? Were you rational the day you pulled your wife's body from the wreckage and vowed to kill every half breed on the planet?" Danby asked

"No, but maybe I should have been!" Ian shouted at him "We have been killing children with our war. Countless innocent women have died and for what? Because we wanted the slaves to remain complacent. Is that why so many people have had to die? Is that how we justify this war?"

"That is exactly how we justify it! The half breeds are like cockroaches, if we allow them to live now, they will outnumber us all. Then we will become their slaves." Danby shouted back

"If this continues none of us will be alive to become their slaves." Ian pointed out

"That may be, but none of them will survive either." Danby said coldly

"So, we will go extinct, instead of learning how to live together?" Ian asked

"If we must." Danby said

"That is insane, you understand that right?" Ian asked

"That is the human way, Ian." Danby said and shrugged unbothered by the idea of all of them dying

"Call the Twins, they must know something." Ian said and stormed out of the room

Caspian watched as the changeling was born. As it drew its first breath, the mother drew it's last. Caspian took the body of the mother and threw it into the lava field. He held the tiny changeling as the body was slowly consumed and contemplated the madness of it all. He felt a tear slide down his cheek and quickly caught it. He let it absorb back into his body, entire planets could be created from his tears.

He walked back and began to carefully clean the newborn changeling. The tiny creature snuggled against seeking a warmth and comfort he did not possess. He knew the changelings could become dangerous if they ever imprinted on a mother that truly loved them. There would be nothing the changeling would not do. The changelings were created to destroy planets, if Caspian set them free. Cree would burn into their skin the secret words, meant to control them. Only one had ever been called forth by the secret words and it had destroyed the planet of the Titans. Pandora had spoken the forbidden words and brought revenge down on the lover who had betrayed her. She had then made a pact with Cree to find his soul, in every life he lived and kill him again. Pandora would not be satisfied until his soul was annihilated.

Cree grabbed the creature from Caspian roughly and it mewled in fear. Cree was not moved by its fear, in fact he enjoyed it. He dipped his finger into the hot lava and began to burn the secret words into its skin. The tiny changeling screamed in pain and Caspian waited for it to be over. He knew if he showed concern for it, Cree would only make the torture last longer. Cree loved Caspian's pain above all else. Finally, Cree shoved the screaming creature back at Caspian.

"I don't like how this one looks." Cree said looking at it in disgust

"It almost resembles a puppy, don't you think?' Caspian

asked inspecting it closer

"I would say more like a mole." Cree disagreed

"Why do you think the Source makes them different every time?" Caspian asked

"Probably, because he is so stupid, he forgets the way looked before." Cree said cruelly

Just then they felt the thundering footsteps, that shook the ground beneath them. They both looked up to see the giant man, who was the Source of all Life.

"Who is stupid Cree?" he asked as he closed the distance between them

Cree looked up in fear "I was speaking of Caspian." he stammered

The Source looked at Caspian and nodded in agreement "He is very stupid, I agree."

Caspian just stared at him. He did not fear the Source, the way Cree did. Caspian knew what he really was, but Cree could not access that memory from him.

"You have made a new changeling." Caspian said to him

The Source leaned down to inspect it closely "Yes, but it isn't right. I need something different." he told him

"For what?" Caspian asked

The Source stood up straight and stuck his tongue out at Caspian "Wouldn't you like to know." he taunted childishly

Caspian simply stared at him and shook his head.

"Where have you two been?" the Source asked them

"We have been to Fae, Huma and Earth." Caspian told him

"What were you doing on Earth?" the Source asked

"Killing dinosaurs." Caspian reported

"You two leave Earth alone! I don't care where else you go, but stay away from there." he commanded them angrily

"What is so special about earth?" Caspian asked, already knowing the answer

"None of your business, Caspian! Do you both understand me?" he bellowed at them

"We understand." Cree said meekly, but Caspian only nodded

After he had left Cree turned on Caspian angrily "Why do you always provoke him?" he asked

"You are the one who called him stupid, not me. Besides I am not afraid of him, the way you are." Caspian said

"I am not afraid of him, but you would do well to remember he is the only thing that can destroy us. His whims are like those of a maniac and we are not safe when he is near." Cree reminded him

"No brother, you are the only one he can destroy. You would do well to remember that." Caspian told him coldly

Cree snatched the changeling from Caspian and snapped its neck mercilessly. He flung the tiny corpse on the ground at Caspian's feet and laughed at Caspian's horrified look.

"You do not exist without me!" he warned him and then tilted his head hearing something in the distance "Come, the humans call for us." he said and waved in their doorway

Only Cree could ever hear the call to them. No one ever

called Caspian's name.

CHAPTER 13

Cree stood staring down at the azurite, not at all surprised it had lost its glow. He had been the one to give the azurite it's unnatural glow in the first place. Even queen Amme had been shocked and she was a hard one to trick. Everyone thought he was in quiet contemplation of this problem, as he stood there silently. The truth was he was basking in amusement at this group of fools. Since the very first being was brought into existence, they all shared the same flaw. All of them would hold a secret desire in their hearts. Power, love, beauty, revenge, it was all the same to him. They all thought he would keep his word and he always did, but never in the way they thought they had agreed to. The only smart ones, were the ones who refused his offers and there were very few of those.

"It must be the fae energy that powers it." he finally told them

"So, we must return to the planet?" Danby asked annoyed at the thought

Cree shook his head sadly "I wish it were that simple. It is not the planet that powers them, but the dark fae herself."

"So, she tricked us!" Danby said outraged at the idea

"Perhaps, but it is more likely she did not know. She is blind to how powerful she really is." Cree reassured him

"What do we do now?" Ian asked

"She must be brought here. It is the only way to power your

weapons." Cree said and shrugged

"She will never agree to that." Ian said dejectedly

"Leave that problem to me." Cree told them

"You promised us the war would be over already! If we wait much longer, there will be no one alive to fight." Danby said

Cree stared at him, not liking his insolent tone "If there is no one alive to fight, then the war would indeed be over. There are many ways to end a war." he replied icily

"Perhaps, you could hold peace talks, to buy yourselves some time." Caspian interjected

When Cree nodded in agreement, Caspian was surprised. He had expected a murderous glare from him, instead Cree smiled that maniacal smile of his and said "Excellent idea!"

"You want us to beg the half breeds for peace?" Danby said sickened by the very idea of it

"No, I want you to buy yourselves some time, while I convince queen Amme to help. She will not be easily moved by your plight. It will take every cleverness I have to convince her." Cree said

"May I suggest that Danby not be involved in the peace talks. He tends to have a hard time controlling his emotions." Caspian said offering advice

Once again Cree nodded in agreement "Quite right! Ian should be the voice of reason in this situation."

"How long do you need?" Ian asked them

"Three days should be sufficient." Cree told him

"I will send a messenger now, excuse me gentleman." Ian said and felt a flood of relief as he left the room, perhaps the war could end peacefully after all

"Keep a close watch on him." Cree whispered to Danby, sowing seeds of distrust "Beautiful women seem to have a way of swaying his allegiance and I hear the leader of the half breeds is quite striking."

Danby opened his mouth to protest, but realized Cree was right. He had already been charmed by Amme, even defending her at times. Ian was weak when it came to women. So, he simply nodded in acknowledgment of the advice. He would keep a close eye on Ian and he would take power if it came to that.

"Are you sure she will come?" Danby asked skeptically

"I am very persuasive; you need not worry. I will deliver the dark fae and your war will end." Cree said and clapped him on the back

Cree turned to leave with Caspian and called back to Danby over his shoulder "Make sure all of your missiles are gathered here. She will be short on patience when the time comes, so make everything ready for her."

Amme walked along the beach in the soft moonlight. She saw something in the distance and could not believe her eyes. The Twins were walking slowly towards her. She felt anger well up inside of her, how dare they come to her home world. Then she remembered what Caspian had shown her and steeled herself for the deal she was about to make. The darkness inside of her began buzzing and reminded her to stay calm. Cree waved at her cheerily at her when he saw her. She stopped walking and let them come to her.

"I did not invite you here." she said rudely when they were finally in earshot

"No, but your great grandfather did! How do you think your family came to sit on the throne?" he asked

"He made a deal with you for the throne?" Amme asked surprised by the knowledge

"Men have made deals for far less." Caspian told her

"I once had someone make a deal with me for a single loaf of bread." Cree informed her proudly

"Why did you just not give it to them, if they were so desperate?" Amme asked disgusted by the thought

"Because nothing in life comes for free, dark fae. Everything has a price, even kindness." he told her

"I do not know how you could give kindness Cree, when it is obvious to me you have never possessed it." Amme told him

Cree shrugged unconcerned "I give only what is asked of me, nothing more."

"Why are you here? Our deal is concluded." she asked done with the small talk

"The humans need your help, once again." Cree told her seriously

"No." Amme said abruptly

"You have not even heard how yet." Cree said

"I do care what they need, the answer is no." she said sternly

"Even if your own husband's soul is in danger?" Cree asked vaguely trying to evoke her curiosity

"Did you really think I did not recognize his soul among the humans you sent?" she laughed

Cree squinted his eyes at her "What a clever young fae you are. His soul is in danger though." he said holding back his anger at her

"So what?" she said confused as to why he would think she cared

"So, you can save him." Cree offered

"Alyks's soul has died before and it will die again, you fool." she said becoming angry at him "A soul must die and be reborn, that is its fate. I have never interfered before and I will not interfere now. His fate is not mine to choose, we may only choose our own."

Cree let his face become blank at her words. If she could not be tricked by using her husband, then perhaps she would be moved by her daughter. She had shown interest in her once, maybe she would again.

"As you wish dark fae, I can see your heart will not be moved by this. I can only hope his daughter feels differently." he told her

"Gaea?" she asked and felt fear begin in the pit of her stomach

"Who else? Unless you have another daughter, I do not know about?" he replied sarcastically

"Leave Gaea alone!" she demanded and the dark energy rose up in her and began to blow the wind around them

Cree held up his hand and the wind stopped instantly "Do not try to use your power against me dark fae!" he commanded

The dak energy shrank back inside of her at the sound of his anger. She felt alone for the first time in centuries, so long had the dark energy protected her. Now she stood under the gaze of the Twins and she understood the limitations of her own power. She knew now what must be done to keep Gaea safe.

"If I help the humans, you must leave Gaea alone. I do not want you to ever speak to her again." Amme said

"Is that all?" Cree asked amused

"No, I do not even want you on the same planet as her. If someone calls you to a planet she is on, you must ignore the call. Your paths must never cross again." Amme told him

"Deal." he agreed

"Until the end of time! Until Gaea and the universe she exists in no longer exist." she added

"Anything else?" he asked becoming annoyed

"No, that will do. What do you need of me?" she asked

"I want every weapon the humans have detonated." he said

"How will that save Alyks's soul?" she asked

"It won't, but you yourself already said you did not care about that." he reminded her

"I don't want you on my planet anymore either." she said trying to add a caveat

Cree opened his hands palm up, dejectedly and said "I'm afraid that would require an entirely different deal. One favor is traded for another, never more. I may be limited to what realms and time loops I can access, but every planet is already open to me. That convenience I will not barter for." he informed her

"What is a realm or a time loop?" Amme asked curiously

Cree gave her a malicious smile "That is something, you need never concern yourself with dark fae." he informed her

Caspian stared at them both as they spoke. How many times had he seen this exact scene play out between them? Amme always trying to save Gaea, Cree always making her destroy Huma. It always ended the same way, except this time a human housed Alyks's soul. Never before had this happened. The Source was making the smallest of changes, but why? He was obviously trying to change something in this storyline, but Caspian could not figure out what it was. Caspian decided in that moment, if the Source wanted to change the outcome, then he would help. He would make one tiny change to this whole scenario, it was after all, his true purpose.

"Do we have a deal then?" asked Cree

"We do." Amme said sealing her own fate

Cree clapped his hands together excitedly "Excellent! Shall we leave now?" he asked

Amme shook her head "No, I must inform Frederick before I leave. Thelry must always have a leader in my absence."

"Then let us meet on Huma." Cree offered

"I will be there, send me the coordinates." she replied

"Why do you never use your doorway fae?" Caspian asked curiously

How could Amme explain that when she flew in a ship, she felt Alyks with her. That if she closed her eyes, she could smell the faintest scent of him. That as she rode through the pure silence of space, she could hear his voice in the distance. That only when she was flying alone, did her heart feel not so alone. That in these moments, she knew peace for the briefest of time. None of this would she ever share with anyone.

"That is none of your concern." she finally answered, but Caspian had felt her emotion and now understood.

He simply bowed to her and said "Until we meet again, dark fae." and turned to leave

"Two days." Cree ordered her and followed Caspian

Amme knocked lightly on Frederick's door and entered his rooms. She found him by the fireplace as usual. He spent most of his time near the fire now and Amme knew that when they began to feel the cold all of the time, death was near.

"How old are you now, Frederick?' she asked

"I am sixty-eight." he said patiently

"I suppose we will have to start training your son soon, to take over your duties." she said

Frederick laughed "My son had been training since he was twenty-five, grandmother. He is ready to take over my duties and in fact had already taken over all of my public ones." he told her

Amme felt embarrassed at the oversight on her part. Long ago she had stopped attending most public functions. Now she could only be seen when a prince was named publicly. Her grandsons were the face of the crown and she had long ago given away that responsibility gladly.

"Of course! How could I have forgotten?' she said

"You are busy running a galaxy grandmother, you need not concern yourself with the mundane tasks of the household or public duty." he told her gently

Amme stared into the fire and said "I did once though."

"Did what?" Frederick asked

"Concerned myself with the household. I oversaw the nannies and chose only the finest. I approved the menus and planned public events. I even checked in on the kitchen staff. I wonder when I stopped?' she said

"Long ago, I assume. It has always been this way in my lifetime." he told her frankly

"Who oversees it all now?" she asked curiously

"My son's wife has taken over the duty, since my own wife died." he told her

"What are their names?' she asked realizing she truly did not know

"My son is Lucian and his wife is named Catherine. The people of the kingdom truly love them." he told her proudly

"Do they?' she asked "How do the people feel about me Frederick?' she asked

Frederick cleared his throat nervously "They appreciate all you do for them Queen Amme. You keep them safe and our food stores full." he reported

"I do not even remember the last time I was among them. I do not attend their celebrations or even address them anymore. I was once a great queen, taught by the finest. I walked among the people and laughter filled the hallways of this palace. Now it is like a tomb for my descendants." she said sadly

"Life must change for all of us. It is the very purpose of it grandmother. The hallways are still filled with laughter, only you have become deaf to it. The people of the kingdom still hold celebrations, only you are absent from them. At night we sit in the dining room and generations of us have dinner together. Only you do not eat with us. The palace feels like a tomb to only you, because all of the dead you once loved still roam the hallways with you. Your gift of perpetual youth has become your curse." he told her wisely

"Do you really believe that?" she asked shocked

"I do." he said bluntly "Who were the two men down on the beach with you?' he asked changing the subject

"I must leave again." she answered ignoring the question

"For how long?" he asked

"Not long, a day or two." she said

"I shall keep everything running smoothly in your absence." he reassured her

She stood up to leave "Perhaps, when I return you and Lucian should join me for dinner." she suggested

"That is a wonderful idea." he said, knowing she would forget the offer

When he was young, he had tried so hard to make her love him. He and his twin brother Roderick would follow her everywhere she went. Hoping she would take the tiniest bit of interest in them. When Roderick became sick, Frederick was sure she would come. Together they had waited for her to come, as Roderick grew sicker and sicker. They thought she would come and offer even the smallest bit of comfort to them., but she never came. One day after Roderick had died, she saw him walking alone down the hallway. When she noticed him and asked where his friend was, it took a minute before Frederick realized she was asking about his brother. It was in that moment he had realized he would never matter to her. He thought to himself for all of her beauty, she was the ugliest person he had ever met. He had hated her every moment of his life since then.

Amme turned in the doorway "Good bye Frederick." she called to him

"Good bye." he called back

CHAPTER 14

Ian walked up the hill, to the spot Miori had agreed to meet him. As he crested the top, he saw the destruction below. What had once been a city teeming with life, was now rubble. Broken pieces of marble and concrete piled up where building had once stood. Stray dogs roamed the streets in packs, looking for food. He wondered if they still waited for their dead owners.

"The enormity of it takes your breath away, doesn't it?' a voice beside him asked

"It seems senseless." he answered honestly

"The destruction or the death?' Miori asked

"Both." he answered

"Why have you called me here?' she asked

Ian drew in his breath to give her some false speech about peace. As he looked down at the chaos below him, he knew that he would never know peace again. None of them would. What they done and witnessed could never be forgotten. Even when the cities were rebuilt, the memory of this would never be forgotten. The images of men, women and children screaming as they dying, would never leave any of them. All of their souls damaged in a way that could never be healed. His own soul so weary from this fight, that he no longer remembered why he fought. He was too tired to lie anymore, too tired to even pray.

"I am here to distract you, so my people can use their weapons against you. So, we can win a war, that none of us can truly win." he said

Miori was to stunned to respond at first. She had expected them to come begging for a truce. They were losing this war, their ranks depleted. Yet, they would still not surrender. She had expected negotiations to begin months ago. They could not win against magic and still they refused to give up.

"All we ever wanted was to be treated equally." she finally said

"I know." Ian admitted

"Then why did we have to fight a war, for this simple desire?" She asked desperate for an answer

"To you it is a simple request, but that is not the way of humans." he said

"Why not though? Other societies live this way, where everyone is equal. Why can't it be this way on Huma?" she asked

Ian shrugged not knowing the answer "I believe we are broken somehow. We feel the need to dominate everything and everyone around us and nothing can erase that desire." he admitted

"So, you will kill us all, including yourselves, rather than live in peace with us?" she asked

"Yes." he said and began to cry at the realization of their madness "You must leave this place, let us destroy ourselves. It is the only way for you to truly survive. As long as one human exists none of you will be safe." he sobbed

Miori sat quietly and let him weep. His sorrow must be great, to betray his own people in this way. When his tears had finally subsided, she spoke again.

"Why did you fight in this war if it causes you so much

pain." she asked

"My rage kept me blinded to my pain. My wife died in the explosion on the first day. I wanted all of you to die with her. I was consumed by a pain that I couldn't explain. That pain sought refuge in rage." he answered

"What has happened to your rage now?" she asked

Ian took a deep breath to steady himself "I think I finally buried it with her. I stood looking at the hyacinth, as it grew around her ashes. I thought she must finally be at peace now, but then I realized she had already found peace in her death. It was me that had sought peace and I knew in that moment; I would never find it in war. Our dead are the luckiest among us, they found their peace instantly. It is those of us that continue to fight, that suffer." he explained

"It was me that day that caused the explosion that killed your wife." Miori confessed

"Why?' he asked desperate to understand his own tragedy

"We lived like animals, on the outskirts of your cities. Punished only because our bloodline contained magic. Punished for something none of us could control. Maybe, we could have continued to live that way, if we would have been left alone. What the soldiers wanted from us was so much more though. They could not be content to take our freedom and dignity. They wanted to kill our spirit, in essence they wanted to destroy our souls. They came to the camps at night and they took it, in any way they saw fit. My people were so broken, they accepted this as their fate, instead of the torture it truly was. Even when they submitted it was not enough to satisfy their cruel appetites. One night as I saw my own mother being brutalized, I understood it would never be enough for them. Some men can never satisfy their desires, no matter how much they feed them. Like a cancer it grows inside of them, feeding from the pain of others. My mother's only crime had been to fall in love with a man from Cala. For this she was punished endlessly on Huma. If she had not returned to Huma seeking permission to marry him, her life and mine would have been different. No one would punish me on Cala for having magic. Men would not freely brutalize my mother there. I saw the soldiers face who was hurting my mother and it burned into my brain.

On the day your wife died, we were protesting peacefully. Then the tall soldier with the red hair who had dragged my mother through the dirt, struck the old man beside me with his gun. I looked into his eyes and all I saw there was hatred. I knew in that moment he would never stop hurting my people and I snapped. The power within me built up into its own rage, consuming my pain. Before I knew it the city was exploding all around me. I did not mean to kill your wife, but I cannot lie to you now, when you stand here and tell me your own truth." she explained

Ian stood silently, processing what she had just said. She had described Danby perfectly. Had Danby really been the cause of this war? He knew Danby and some of the other soldiers liked to go into the camps on occasion. When Ian had voiced his concern about it, they had all reassured him they were just blowing off some steam and no one was being hurt. Deep down Ian had known the truth though, and he choose to ignore it. He had known what they really did and he had done nothing to stop them. He was their commanding officer and he had turned a blind eye. Miori was wrong to think they had suffered like animals, because even animals were treated better in Huma.

"You did not have to tell me this." he finally said

"Truth must be shared equally; it is my fault your wife died." she answered

He shook his head "No, it is mine. The soldier you speak of was under my command. I knew what he and the others came here to do and I did nothing. My silence was his permission." he told her humiliated at the admission

"What do we do now?" Miori asked as the sun began to sink into the horizon

"Take your people and leave this planet. I will tell my people you have agreed to a truce, it should buy you a day or two." he said

"Can't we save it now? Surely the two of us can figure out a way to make this stop." She pleaded

Ian shook his head "Men like my friend Danby are not the exception to the rule, they are the rule. We must destroy it; it is the only way for your people to survive. The weapons we have designed will kill everything on this planet. You must leave before it is too late." he warned

"Where will we go?" Miori asked desperately "What planet will accept this many refugees?"

"Perhaps Cala, you could seek out your father." he suggested

It was then that she remembered Cree's offer to her. The planet Fae was empty and they could start over there. They could build a society where everyone was free.

"I am truly sorry for your wife." she told him

"I am truly sorry about your life." he said and she nodded "Go now, gather your people and leave this place. I will buy you some time." he told her and began to cry again as she walked away

Cree helped her to secure some ships and came to oversee the loading. The oldest among them would stay behind. If they all disappeared it would not go unnoticed. They would keep the humans distracted until the weapons went off.

As the last ship was being loaded, Miori stood next to Cree "How can I ever thank you?" she asked him

"I need no thanks, someday I will come to you for a favor. You may repay me then." he told her

"You are sure we may inhabit Fae?" she asked

"Of course, I am! It belongs to me now; I made a deal for it." he told her

Cree clapped his hands together as she watched the final ship leave "I have done it again brother!" he exclaimed joyfully

"Done what?" Caspian asked

"Made the perfect deal." Cree replied

CHAPTER 15

Amme set the course for Huma and then wandered through the empty ship. The ship was positively ancient, a relic of long ago. She had kept it maintained and repaired for ten thousand years. The newest ships with the most advanced technology did not interest her. This is the ship that Alyks had flown those many years ago. This is the ship that had once taken her to discover her own powers on Fae. This was the ship that had Gaea to her own fate with Sisue. When they had been returning from Fae, after they left Gaea, Amme had discovered a small blanket left behind. Amme pulled it from a drawer now and help it up. It was old and faded now, the fabric tattered, but when she buried her face in it, she could still smell Gaea. She was sure that if anyone else had sniffed the tiny blanket, they would smell nothing. Only she was left to recognize the smell of the tiny baby. She knew if Alyks were here, he would be able to smell it also.

Instead of returning to to the drawer like she normally did, she tucked it into her dress. She did not understand why she did this, but felt comfort in having it next to her. She had always followed her desires and never stopped to question them. Later when the world finally grew quiet around her, she would finally understand that fate had intervened that day. It would not be until much later, that she would come to this understanding.

As she flew over Fae, she saw five ships entering into its orbit. She became so outraged by this; she almost changed her course. Instead, she decided she would deal with it after she had helped the humans. Her priority was to keep Gaea safe from

Cree. The trespassers to Fae, would be dealt with when she was done. She assumed it was the humans, they had shown to keen an interest in her planet. First though she must help them kill one another.

She almost laughed at the irony of it all. Not since the Titans, had a species been so intent on destroying themselves. The Titans own children had turned on them, having decided they wanted a new way of life. The system the Titans had set up did not satisfy them. They had destroyed their entire planet this way, with only Pandora surviving. It was a tale told to children at bedtime, so they could be warned.

If the humans were not careful, they would meet the same fate. Soon enough she saw Huma come into view. She regretted the day she and Alyks had granted permission for Primis to use the small planet. If not for Primis and the humans, Cree would have never known about Gaea. As the ship lowered onto the planet, she saw the destruction everywhere. They had destroyed everything just to punish one another. She could not imagine how they found the will to continue to live in this environment. It would take at least three generations before the planet was rebuilt.

Miori stepped off the ship and breather the air in deeply. Their own planets air had become so polluted, it was hard to breathe there. She took in the wild, pristine landscape in awe. She had been told that Huma had once looked like this, but never in her imagination had she been able to think of anything like this. Her imagination could never conjure this kind of beauty. A herd of wild horses grazed nearby, while she saw cows in the distance. None of the animals feared their presence.

Miori's mother threw her arms around her daughter "We may actually eat meat in our lifetime!" she said excitedly

Miori looked at the cows warily "We will not begin killing

as soon as we land. We have enough supplies to last until we set up a system here." she chastised

Her mother looked at her shocked "We must eat Miori. It is why animals were made." she reminded her

Miori turned to all of the refugees now "We will eat only what we have brought, until further notice. Right now, let's begin making a temporary encampment for the night. Tomorrow we will form groups and begin to sort out the issues we face. That tower in the distance is off limits to any of us." she ordered

Miori's people nodded and slowly began setting up temporary shelter. They could not know they had left a dangerous situation, for a fate far worse. Tonight, they were all filled with hope for a brighter future.

Ian and Danby sat across from one another, quietly sipping their drinks. The tension between them was thick, although neither of them spoke a word. They waited for Amme to come and fix their azurite.

Danby watched Ian closely. He had been acting differently since he had returned from the peace talk. Perhaps, Cree was right about him and beautiful girls were in fact his weakness. Had he been so easily charmed by a half breed? Danby couldn't be sure, to him the half breeds were nameless and faceless, like cockroaches. He had been raised in a family that took pride in the purity of their bloodline. Danby was a descendant of the first humans, made by Primis to be genetically perfect. As soon as he was old enough, he had signed up for the military, to defend this perfect bloodline.

In fact, the military was where he had met Ian. Both of the young soldiers had formed an instant bond. Ian had once been as wild and reckless as Danby, if not more so. Ian's wife had tamed his wild streak though and he had become less fun after he had gotten married. It was one of the reasons Danby had vowed to never marry. He would never allow a female to control him and tame him.

After she had died though, Ian had become ruthless in his hatred of the half breeds. Danby thought he had become even more zealous than himself, which was hard to accomplish. He had loved fighting beside the blood thirsty version of Ian that had emerged. It was Fae, that he had lost that edge and Danby blamed the witch queen for that. When the war was over, he vowed to find some way to make her pay.

Ian stared at Danby, with the same intensity. Miori's words would not leave his mind. Even in their earliest days together, he had known Danby could take things too far. Many times, he had gone along with Danby, just to ensure he never took things too far. When he had met his wife, he had begun to focus less on Danby. Left unchecked, Danby had become more dangerous than Ian ever could have imagined. After his wife had died, Ian welcomed the blood thirsty Danby. He had needed someone who could match his own level of rage. Together they had been unstoppable and had waged war with a vigor unmatched by any of the other soldiers. What Ian had never stopped to consider was where had Danby's own rage come from. He knew his own had come from the death of his wife, but Danby had suffered no loss. It had taken losing his wife for Ian to become filled with so much hate. Why was Danby so consumed with hate? Why had Ian turned a blind eye so long ago, to the hatred that Danby did not hide from anyone. Had the actions of one man, really caused a war? Was it because of Danby that his wife had died?

"Do you remember those nights when you and the other soldiers would get drunk and raid the encampments?" Ian asked breaking the tense silence

Danby recalled many of those nights and smiled at the memory of them "Yes." he answered

"What did you do when you went there?" Ian asked wanting to somehow wipe the smile off of Danby's face

Danby looked at Ian, knowing what he was alluding to "We did what men do." he smirked

"What do men do?' he asked through clenched teeth, knowing now everything Miori had said was true

Danby winked at Ian "You had a wife, Ian; you know exactly what men do."

"On the day of the protest that started the war, where were you Danby?" Ian asked

"I was in the square guarding the half breeds." Danby answered thrown off by the question

Ian gripped his glass tighter in anger "What did you do to them that day?" he asked

Danby's brows furrowed in confusion "What do you mean?" he asked

"What did you do to them!" Ian asked his voice beginning to rise to match his anger

"I kept them in line, exactly like you ordered." Danby said understanding now what Ian was referring to "Or did you forget brother?" he asked laughing

"I did not order you to hurt them." Ian yelled and slammed his fist onto the table

"But you did!" Danby yelled back "Every time you gave us orders or turned a blind eye, you asked us to hurt them. Even if you did not say the words your meaning was very clear. You knew what we were doing and not once did you try to stop us. Your silence was all the command we ever needed." Danby was amused at Ian's outrage

"I did not know you were hurting them." Ian protested

"We both know you did though! You would clap us all on the back and tell us not to cause to much trouble, before we left for the encampments. You would wink at all of us and tell us to have fun. Then you would go home and climb into your warm bed with your wife. You probably never even gave it another thought Ian, until now. So why now Ian? Why does it weigh so heavy on your conscience today?" Danby asked

Ian sat back, realizing Danby was right. He had known and he had done nothing to stop it. Soldiers blowing off steam, he had told himself. No harm had come from those nights. The half breeds had already accepted their fate and made no complaints after this happened. He had gone home and slept soundly, all those nights and he had known every time they were going. Harmless fun, he had reasoned, but it wasn't harmless. It had turned them all into soulless monsters, who enjoyed inflicting terror. Incapable of common decency that was the right of every person, even those with magic.

Ian hung his head in shame "We were wrong Danby. This war is our fault, yours and mine."

"We followed the rules left to us by our creator." Danby reminded him unmoved

"How do we justify what we have done to the half breeds by words left to us long before they even existed? Primis left this planet, before we were even capable of going to other planets. How do we even know he is real or just something made up by first man? How do we continue to follow the rules of a creator we don't even know existed? We carry out atrocities in the name of some God we have never met!" Ian said horrified for the first time at the thought of what he was saying

"We follow his words, because he left them for us. We

follow his guidance to keep ourselves safe, until he returns for us." Danby said reciting the doctrine they had all been raised on

"Do we look safe?" Ian asked stunned "Our planet is on the brink of destruction and for what? For words that have been interpreted in so many ways, so many different times that they aren't even the original anymore? Words that are twisted by powerful men to fit their own agenda? We follow blindly, accepting and never trying to seek their meaning on our own. We just listen as each new spiritual leader that comes into power, twists them to fit their own needs at the time." Ian asked

"So, now on the brink of our victory, you question your faith, Ian?" Danby asked

"Is this your definition of victory? We sit underground in a world that is already destroyed. A world that cannot be fixed in our lifetime, even if the war ends today. Our grandchildren will live among this destruction we have caused. Is that what victory means to you?" Ian asked exhausted by Danby's refusal to acknowledge any wrong doing

"You are unfit to lead anymore, Ian. You have let either the witch or the half breed corrupt you. I am relieving you of your command." Danby told him, tired of allowing his weakness to be given a voice

Ian looked up at him coldly "You can try." he challenged

Danby looked at him and without hesitation shoved the table forward towards him. Ian's chair toppled over backwards from the force of it. Before he had time to pick himself up from the floor, Danby was on top of him raining down blows. Ian managed to slide himself backwards with his elbows. He pulled up both of his legs towards his chest and kicked with all his force. The blow to Danby's chest sent him flying backwards and he fell onto the table. The table was crushed beneath the force of his weight and splintered as it broke. Ian scrambled to his feet, as Danby disentangled himself from the wood. Blood from his eyebrow trickled down into Ian's eye, leaving his sight blurry. Danby screamed a primal scream of rage at Ian as he stood up and kept low as he lunged at Ian. The breath was knocked from Ian's lungs as Danby caught him in the torso and drove him back into the wall. Ian pounded his fists into Danby's back, but Danby help his grip on him. Ian felt himself close to losing consciousness, as he struggled to draw air into his lungs.

Amme walked in with the Twins and found them both this way. She flicked her hand and Danby flew across the room and hit the opposite wall. He crumpled to the ground and did not move. Ian slumped down and drew in deep gasping breaths. Cree walked slowly across the room to see if Danby was still alive. Caspian took the opportunity while Cree had his back turned to change this story. He touched Ian on the shoulder and waited to see what outcome this one small change would have.

CHAPTER 16

Ian looked up at Amme and said "Please help me."

Amme looked at him in shock, immediately recognizing his voice. The despair in his eyes and the desperation in his voice, told her what she saw was real.

"Alyks?" she stammered still unsure

"Amme, please help me." he said again and began to cry

Amme rushed to him, while Cree turned to glare at Caspian "What have you done?" he asked with venom in his voice

"Exactly, what I was created to do." Caspian replied vaguely, finally understanding what the Source wanted him to do

Amme bent down to face Alyks, who had buried his face in his own hands. She gently pulled at them until their eyes finally met. As soon as she saw his eyes, she knew his soul had awoken.

"How is this possible?" she whispered, feeling her own tears begin to burn her eyes

Alyks shook his head "I do not know love, but I am here." he said and reached up to touch her face

"I have missed you." she said and the first tear slid down her cheek

"Oh, my love, I have missed you to." he said and quickly pulled her into his arms

They held onto one another wordlessly, until Cree

interrupted their peace.

"Yes, yes what a happy reunion!" he said sarcastically "But why are you here?" he yelled angrily at Alyks

Amme and Alyks both stood up, but did not let go of one another. Amme was caught off guard at Cree's undeniable anger. His masked had finally slipped and she saw the evil creature he truly was.

Alyks turned to Amme ignoring Cree "You cannot let my soul die in this form or it will be lost until the end of time." he told her desperately, knowing they didn't have much time left

"What do you mean?' She asked confused

"It is corrupted, by that being." he said and pointed at Cree

"How?" she asked

"Primis believes humans are made with the DNA from the heavens. It does not come from the heavens though, it is his. He means to seed the universe with chaos. Once a soul has entered a human form it cannot be sent back to the heavens or it is destroyed. Primis created the underworld until he could figure out a solution. He will never find one though, because he will never discover the truth." Alyks told her

"Is this true?" Amme asked Cree horrified at what he had done

Cree shrugged nonchalantly "What are a few lost souls in the scheme of things?" he asked

Amme turned to Caspian now "Did you know?" she asked

Caspian did not reply, he simply shook his head yes.

"Why did you not stop him?" she yelled at Caspian now

Cree laughed at her anger "He cannot stop me dark fae. He is me and I am him." he cackled

"What?' Amme asked confused

"Tell her Caspian or do you want me to?" Cree asked

Caspian looked down at his feet nervously, wondering how to explain. Should he start at the beginning before Cree or should he just tell the story since Cree's creation? He looked up and began speaking

"He is the embodiment of all that is terrible in me. Once, only I existed alone. Two parts of one being. My pain and loneliness grew so big inside of me, it began to take on a life of its own. Cree is everything that was dark and terrible inside of me." he told her ashamed of what he had created

"I am his darkest thoughts and most terrible desires." Cree said proudly

"He is the monster under my bed, come to life. He is the demon that lived once in my closet." Caspian said

Amme approached Cree and walked around him slowly. Every detail of him perfectly matched Caspian.

"How old were you when this happened?" she asked Caspian

"Just a boy, it was before the universe even existed." he told her "But time is meaningless, I could have already been in existence for a million years in this story. I am infinite."

"What does that mean?' she asked

"I have no beginning and no ending. Only this form is bound to this time line and this Source of all Life." he said knowing this would keep Cree confused

"So, he is your fear, come to life?" Amme asked gently

"I am the embodiment of all his emotions, dark fae. This is not my fear and pain you see; it belongs to the Source. So big it cannot be contained by just one of us. It is like an ocean of pain." he said trying to explain, what she could never understand

"If he is fear and pain, does that make you love and happiness?" she asked trying to grasp it

"It is more complex than that. I am everything left over. There are too many emotions to name, but I am everything he is not." Caspian replied

"Why is the Source of all Life, filled with so much fear and pain?" Alyks asked

Caspian shrugged "I cannot answer that, it is not my place. I can only embody his emotions and desires. I do know that he can kill Cree, but never me. If he ever chose to face his own pain it would destroy Cree." Caspian explained

"How dare you tell them that!" Cree screamed at Caspian

Caspian smirked at Cree "It's not like they can do anything with the information. You have already destroyed the only people who had the ability to reach him."

"Who did he destroy?" Amme asked

"The Titans, of course. His manipulation and trickery caused the destruction of the entire race. They were created to seek out the Source, but alas that would have destroyed Cree. That he would never allow." Caspian told them

"So, none of this will ever stop? Cree will continue to wreak havoc anywhere he pleases, for eternity?" Alyks asked

"I'm afraid so, unless the Source can find a way to confront his own fear. Which, I'm sorry to say, isn't likely to happen."

Caspian told them, leaving out the fact that this story had already been told numerous times

"Which is why you must remove my soul from this body and destroy this planet." Alyks told Amme

"How am I supposed to do that?" Amme turned and asked him in confusion

"You simply pluck it out, dark fae." Cree told her and laughed

Cree had to admit he had been furious when Caspian had awoken Alyks's soul, but he couldn't have predicted this. He was very pleased with how this was playing out. She must sacrifice herself to save Alyks, but she also would have to destroy this planet. Only by allowing the dark energy to completely consume her, would she be powerful enough to pluck his soul and keep it protected.

Caspian knew exactly why Cree was happy. He only saw the destruction of Amme and Huma as the outcome. Caspian saw something else and he had to admit he was intrigued. The usual outcome of this story was that Amme would become so enraged to discover the humans were trying to wipe out magic, she detonated their missiles. In doing so she would destroy Huma, but also always destroyed herself. If she was consumed by the dark energy, Amme's soul would live. Although she would become a part of the dark energy and her form would be lost, she would still exist. The dark energy was also infinite, it could never be destroyed. It was only a slight change to the story, but Caspian finally understood the magnitude of it. The Source was seeking something, without alerting any of the others. No one would take notice of small variations, after all life had a way of creating variations in every story. You cannot stop, what you cannot see! It was the unspoken rule that stories could not be changed. Over and over again the souls were meant to play out the lives they had imagined for themselves. It was their punishment.

"You must let the dark energy consume you completely this time Amme. It is the only way to save his soul." Caspian instructed her

"What will happen when it consumes me?" Amme asked almost afraid of the answer

"You and Alyks will live happily ever after. Isn't that all you have ever really wanted?" Cree asked her

"Your souls will continue to exist, but not in this way dark fae. You will be trapped in the dark energy until the end of time. The life you know now, will cease to exist in every way imaginable." Caspian told her

"And Gaea?" she asked hesitantly

"Cree will still be bound to the deal he made to you as long as your soul exists. I will make sure of that." Caspian reassured her

"Are you sure this is the only way?" Amme asked Alyks

Alyks nodded sadly "It is the only reason I choose to this life. We must save our daughter and stop the humans to save Thelry. They will destroy the entire universe if they are allowed to live, Amme."

Just then Danby came to and sat up. He watched the exchange between the witch and Ian and knew his suspicions had been right. She had corrupted his old friend and now he begged her to destroy the humans, as if he weren't one himself. In a rage he stood up and pulled his knife from his belt.

"You do not need to beg her Ian; I will gladly kill you!" he said and stomped towards them

Neither Alyks or Amme moved at the sound of his voice.

Amme looked deep into his eyes and said "Are you ready my love?"

Alyks nodded and Amme called out to the dark energy. She told it exactly what she needed and then it felt as if she were falling backwards, into nothingness. She felt like she landed into a warm pool of water, in total darkness. Although she could no longer see, she could feel everything. The darkness had once existed with the silver light and the golden light as one. When the souls had begun to take form, they had split into three separate energies. Spreading across the universe, each trying to reunite the souls with their original home. Amme could feel herself filling with power now, a power that longed to be set free within her.

The four men watched as Amme closed her eyes and began to transform. Danby was stopped in his tracks by the sight of it. It began at her feet, a black mist that began to envelop her, until her feet and legs no longer existed. The black mist began to engulf her torso, until only her head remained. As the black mist finished consuming her, a black hand reached out from the mist. The black hand slammed into Ian's chest and pulled out a small golden ball, as his body fell backwards onto the floor dead.

Danby fainted as the mist turned towards him.

Cree held up a hand to stop it and said "I will take care of this one. The bombs are on the floor below."

The black mist that had once been Amme, Queen of Thelry, last of the dark fae, turned for the doorway. Cree waved in their doorway, when the mist was gone and turned to Caspian as he flung Danby's unconscious body over his shoulder "Come brother, my work here is done. The war is most definitely over." he said and laughed as they walked away from Huma.

CHAPTER 17

The dark energy flowed down the stairwell towards the weapon room. It could feel the darkness that the weapons pulsed with. They had been meant to destroy this planet, whether the humans realized it or not. All weapons were meant for destruction. A simple branch from a tree, when picked up could become a weapon. When used in anger, anything was a weapon. This planet was thick with the dark energy of all of their anger and the dark energy absorbed it into itself, becoming more powerful as it consumed all of their rage. The dark energy grew ten times its size, before even reaching the weapons room.

When it reached the weapons room, it flung the doors open from their hinges. The terrified soldiers and scientists ran to the back of the room, terrified of what they saw. The soldiers quickly recovered their senses and began to fire on it. A flurry of bullets was shot, until the soldiers realized it only grew bigger as it absorbed each shot. Once they stopped a face emerged from the mist and shrieked at them. The sound was deafening and caused a painful buzzing in their heads. They covered their ears in agony and fell to their knees.

"Can you stop it?" one of the soldiers yelled to a scientist

"It's magic, I can't stop magic." the scientist yelled back

The face in the black mist began to laugh and speak in an unnatural voice "I am not magic you fools!" it taunted them "I am the destruction of creation. I am the alpha and the omega."

One armed formed from the mist and it swung at the

concrete wall. The entire wall was blown away and the men could see outside. The bright sunlight poured in, blinding them all for a moment. The sound of the metal as it scraped across the floor was unnerving, as all of the weapons turned to face the opening. They all tipped upwards ready to fire.

The face in the mist turned towards the men one last time and spoke "Now you will witness what your terrible creation was meant for, humans." It said and swung its black arm towards the opening.

One by one the missiles shot out and flew into the air. Each making adjustments to land in different locations. When all fifty had reached the same height they hovered in the air, suspended. People all over the planet looked up to see the missiles above them. The black mist waited until a collective horror had settled over the planet. They collective knowledge, that they had created their own destruction. The black arm swung down and released the missiles, simultaneously. A bright flash was all that followed.

As Amme floated through space, trapped inside of the dark mist, she began to cry. She did not understand what she had become, but she knew she would never again have form. She felt cold and alone, until a voice called out to her softly.

"Why do you weep my love?"

"Alyks?" she called out confused without sight

"I am here Amme; you are not alone." he said

"How?" she asked, not even sure how they were talking

"Our souls still exist Amme, they never stop existing." he told her

"How are we speaking?" she asked

"We aren't we are thinking, it is how our souls have always

communicated." he explained

"I don't understand." she said

"You will, dark fae. Our souls are magnificent things made of pure energy. Our thoughts become our voices and our voices become the story we tell. The infinite believed our stories were separate, but only when we combine them does our true power reveal itself." he said softly remembering the lessons he had been taught in the heavens

"Who are the infinite?" Amme asked

"We all are, Amme." he answered

"What is our true power?' she asked

Suddenly a light filled a small room and Amme blinked, looking around in awe. A rocking chair sat in the middle of the room. A small cradle sat next to it. A large window looked out onto the familiar ocean of Thelry. Amme walked over to it and when she turned back to the chair, Alyks stood beside it. Amme let her eyes take in every familiar inch of him. He was not the old man she had lost long ago, he stood now looking the same as the day they met.

He smiled at her "Our true power is our imagination, Amme. Our imaginations have the power of creation in them. Our minds can create new worlds."

Amme crossed the room quickly and fell into his arms. She had no idea where they were, but she knew she was home at last. He held her tightly, until a soft cry came from the cradle.

Amme stepped back and looked at him surprised "Gaea?"

Alyks smiled at her and nodded. Amme walked over to the cradle and peeked down over the edge. Inside the tiny face of her newborn looked up at her. She leaned down and gently picked her up. She walked to the window with her and Alyks wrapped his arms around her waist. He rested his head on her shoulder and stared down at their daughter.

"Is this real?" Amme whispered, frightened that it all might disappear

"Everything we imagine is real, Amme. We exist now in the dark energy, but that doesn't make it less real. The dark energy will keep our souls safe, until time itself resets and we return." he told her

"Return where?" she asked

"To the place where it all began. Where the souls and the energies are all one thing combined. Where we are all the infinite once again." he said

"When will that be?' she asked

"Time does not exist Amme, I cannot know the answer to that." he said

"What about the dark energy?" she asked

"Think of it as a ship that carries us now." he said

"Are we trapped here; can we never go home?" she asked

"Your soul is my home, Amme. We are not trapped here; we have been set free. Everything I have I give to you." he said

She turned to him and said "Your soul is my home, Alyks. Everything I have I give to you." she told him "What will happen to our kingdom? Do you think everyone will be okay?' she asked

"It is no longer our kingdom. We have neither form or possessions. We only have each other and the power to create any life we wish." he said

Amme turned back around and leaned back into him. He was all she had ever really wanted. She saw a familiar planet come into view, through the window now.

"It seems the dark energy is returning to Fae." she said

The black mist floated down onto the planet, where it had rested for a millennium. The smell of campfires hung thick in the air. The sounds of construction had quieted the singing of the birds. The black mist instantly recognized the destruction, humans always brought with them.

Miori looked up, thinking a black cloud was covering the sky. She quickly realized this was no storm cloud coming at them so fast. The black mist gave her an uneasy feeling. She reached out with her mind to discover what it truly was. Immediately she felt the residue of the dark fae, that had once wielded it. She felt the pain of the dark fae and her desperation.

Beyond that she felt the true nature of the dark energy. In it was death, the end of all things. The pain and suffering that all life must experience. Within that pain and suffering was its very essence. Miori knew in that moment that everything must exist, even this terrible energy had its place in the universe.

She saw flashes of what it intended to do to them. It would not let her escape the fate of the other humans, even if they were only half breeds. She saw that it had completely destroyed Huma. It would not destroy this planet though, only them. The dark energy did not care if their fight had been just. It was only interested in the destruction of the humans. It sought only to annihilate their DNA.

She felt her mother's hand slip into hers "What is it Miori?' she asked

Miori squeezed her mother's hand tightly in comfort "It is our death." she replied as the black mist descended down on them all furiously

CHAPTER 18

Cree knocked softly on the door and entered when he heard the old man yell "Come in."

He walked slowly across the room and sat down across from the man "It is done, your queen is dead." he informed him

Frederick let out a sigh of relief "Thank you." he told Cree

"When will you have your coronation?" Cree asked

The old man scoffed at the idea "It is my son, Lucian who will be crowned, not me." he replied

"You made this deal for your son?" Cree asked surprised

"Yes, he deserves to be king. The people have long awaited a new ruler. Queen Amme stopped leading them long ago." Frederick said

"Perhaps, but wouldn't you like a taste of the power the crown offers before you die?" Cree asked

"I was never meant to be a king; I accepted the truth of that long ago. No one will make a finer king then Lucian though, he was born for greatness." Frederick said proudly

"Most men believe they are born for greatness. They are never able to accept their mediocrity." Cree pointed out

"Most men are fools." Frederick quipped "Lucian does not believe he was born for greatness. He believes he was born to serve the people of this kingdom. That is precisely what will make him a great king."

"I truly hope he was worth your betrayal." Cree said hoping to prick at the old man's guilt

Frederick folded his hands together "You may call it a betrayal, but it was necessary." he said unconcerned

"A necessary evil, I am all too familiar with the term. The concept is as old as time itself." Cree said thinking back to how everyone who made a deal with him justified their actions this way

"What is evil though, really? Her reign had to end sometime. At least it has ended when a proper replacement was available." Frederick contemplated the thought

"Have you told him yet?" Cree asked bored by the old man already

"No, I will tell him in the morning. Her flight coordinates clearly show she went to Huma. There will be much to do, he will need his rest tonight." Frederick said anticipating the fervor of events that must take place quickly

"Will you tell him about the part you played to make him king?" Cree asked curiously

"Absolutely not!" Frederick said angrily

Cree looked at him concerned "How will you explain that you have given away Fae? How will you explain the people that you have traded?"

"I have already forged the documents you asked for weeks ago. Queen Amme herself gifted you the planet. As for the people you will take, a document has been readied by her also, giving them to you. In five hundred years when you come to collect them, my son and I will be long dead. He need not be worried about certain details." Frederick replied

"How did you know to have the documents ready?" Cree

asked

"I saw you talking to her on the beach, the night before she left. I know exactly what you are, so I knew the time had come." he answered

Cree leaned forward in his chair, closer to Frederick. He loved when beings gave him a new name, adding to the many he already had.

"What am I?' he asked excitedly

"You are the devil. I have made a deal with the devil." Frederick said and gulped at the meaning of his words

Cree laughed with pure joy at the description "Do you mean the fallen angel?" he asked recalling the story

"That is exactly what I mean." Frederick stammered, not understanding Cree's reaction

Cree clapped his hands together and sat back delighted "Then the devil I shall be!" he exclaimed

"I do not understand your happiness. You already know what you are." Frederick said becoming unnerved

Cree's face turned serious "Of course, I know what I am you fool! What never ceases to surprise me is people like you. Do you know that of all the people who have made a deal with me, Queen Amme was the only who did so for an unselfish reason? She did not seek power like you or control like Primis. Even the half breeds sought their deal for a selfish reason. She sought only the safety and a glimpse of her daughter. You would call me evil, but you are the one who made a deal for the death of your grandmother. All so you and your son could control the throne."

"Queen Amme did not have a daughter." Frederick said growing concerned by the information

"Oh, but she does! She has a very powerful daughter, more powerful than even her. She gave her life for this daughter. She must be very special indeed if the dark fae gave her life willingly." Cree said and winked "Do you wonder if her daughter ever discovers the truth if she will come for her birthright? Do you think she would take her place on the throne and punish those responsible for the death of her mother?' Cree asked feigning shock at the idea

"You will protect us if that happens?' Frederick asked growing concerned

Cree stood up abruptly "I am afraid that was not part of the deal we made." he said sadly "Now I will take my documents and leave. Our business is concluded."

Frederick stood up in a panic "You must protect us! I have given you a planet and two hundred of our people. Sure, you can extend some courtesy to this situation."

Cree turned on him in disgust "You wanted Queen Amme dead! I wanted the planet Fae and one hundred of your strongest men and one hundred of your most beautiful women. You agreed to those terms Frederick, do not beg me to amend the agreement now."

"Then let us make another deal." Frederick said desperately

"You have nothing I want." Cree told him

"I have an entire kingdom, surely you can think of something." Frederick begged

"You have nothing, your son has an entire kingdom. In fact, I suspect he will replace you as royal advisor quickly. You are nothing more than an old man, who has used up all of his bargaining chips." Cree said

Frederick retrieved the papers from his desk. What had he done? He had never known Amme had a daughter and if she lived, she must also be ageless. Maybe, that is why she went to Fae so often. Perhaps, her daughter lived there and soon she find out Cree now owned the planet. What would happen if she came to avenge her mother? Everything he had done, would be ruined. His children and grandchildren could lose the throne. He had damned them all. It was his fault his entire family now stood on the brink of destruction.

"Do not worry yourself old man. Someday, your son will call to me and I will answer." Cree reassured him mockingly

Caspian sat on a hot rock at the edge of the abyss. He stared at Danby, who laid in a stasis chamber. Cree was keeping him, but Caspian could not understand why. He felt the thundering footsteps of the Source, but did not look up. The Source lowered himself onto the rock next to Caspian and looked at the stasis chamber.

"Is that yours?" he asked Caspian

Caspian shook his head "No, it's Cree's."

"Well, that is new!" the Source exclaimed delighted "I have never seen it before. Do you remember seeing it before?" he asked

"No, I have never seen it. In fact, I am starting to notice a lot of little things I have never seen before." Caspian told him

"Are you?" the Source asked curiously

"Yes, and I am beginning to become concerned." Caspian told him

"I am curious myself." the Source said innocently

"So, you are not the one making them?' Caspian asked

"Of course not! If the others found out I was making changes, I would be in big trouble, you know." he protested

"Who do you think is making them then?" Caspian asked

"Probably Cree, he is always making trouble. You can't control the changes chaos makes, though." the Source reasoned

"Do you want me to stop him?" Caspian whispered

"No, I want you to help him. Only you can see the changes, he can't. Nothing to noticeable, you understand. Like what you did when you woke up Alyks's soul. Small changes, until we can create what we need." the Source whispered back conspiratorially

"What do we need?" Caspian asked

"Immortals." the Source said excitedly

"You have Aiden though, why do you need more?" Caspian asked

"I need a special one Caspian. Cree can change the story without anyone noticing, but you must watch the changes," the Source explained

"You are looking for them, aren't you?" Caspian asked, finally understanding

"They can't find me Caspian, so I must find them." the Source said sadly

"I will do my best." Caspian reassured him

"It is all in your hands Caspian. You will know when to make the changes, when the time presents itself. Just like you knew to wake up Alyks." the Source said

"I'm not sure how I did that though? Why did waking up Alyks's soul make any difference?' Caspian asked

"Gaea must play her part and the dark energy must play a part. Only a powerful family can keep the new Source safe. Only an immortal can defy the will of the Infinite. All these things must combine like an intricate spider web and no one is better at weaving a web, then Cree."

"I still do not see how it will all come together?" Caspian said

"That is precisely why it will work. The outcome is so entangled in the story, no one can see it. Not even Cree can see what he is doing. He thinks he only creates chaos, but it is in that chaos that the new story hides!" the Source said

CHAPTER 19

The Twins walked in to find Primis, sitting the exact same way they had left him. He sat looking forlorn and shot Cree a look of pure hatred.

"How dare you show your face to me, after you let Huma be destroyed!" he yelled at him

Cree held up both of his hands "Settle down old friend!" he said trying to calm the Lagorian

"You lied to me. I thought you were my friend." Primis said accusingly

Caspian sat down, curious to see how this would play out.

"I am your friend. I have brought you wonderful news." Cree defended himself and sat down

"No news you bring could make up for the fact that you let them all die." Primis said forlornly

"I know you loved them like your own children, my friend." Cree said soothingly "They struggled without your guidance and wisdom."

Caspian rolled his eyes at the dramatics that Cree was stooping to "Yes, how could they have known the weapons they built would be so powerful." He said mocking them both

Cree looked at him and nodded sadly in agreement. Caspian almost burst out laughing at the absurdity of it all. The humans had known exactly what they had built. They just believed they could control the destruction. Either that or they didn't really care. Caspian would not be surprised at the answer either way.

"All is lost now." Primis cried out again and buried his face in his hands

"Not yet, it isn't." Cree told him excitedly "The universal council has agreed to let you try again."

Primis looked up shocked "What?' he asked disbelievingly

"I spoke on your behalf." Cree told him leaving out all of the deals he had made for this to happen

"What did they say?" Primis asked

"Your punishment still stands, but it has been suspended indefinitely. You will lead a group of scientists and you will be allowed to bring the humans to life once more. You can finally fix them!" Cree said pleased with himself

"How? Where? When?' Primis blurted in his excitement

"The planet Earth has just experienced an extinction event, so it sits empty. It will have to be terra formed to support human life, but that gives you time to work with the DNA again. You will work closely with the other scientists, to create the perfect humans. The universal council was so impressed with your ability to create a life form, they feel your species deserves another chance. It will allow their own scientists to learn to create a new species from you." Cree said lying flawlessly

In fact, the universal council had been outraged by Primis's secret experiment. It had taken Cree much persuasion and a few deaths, to convince them otherwise. Caspian had merely watched as Caspian manipulated everyone to do his will. At first Caspian could not understand why, but then it became clear. Gaea sat on the team of scientists and it was her planet that had been chosen to house the humans. He had made the deal to leave her alone, but he was intent on manipulating everything around her. It was the grey area, that Cree could always find. He was bound by creation to never be near her, but that didn't stop him from sabotaging her from afar.

"When do we begin?" Primis asked

"Immediately old friend. We have come to escort you off this planet." Cree said and stood up

"Let's go! I want to get started." Primis aid heading for the door

"I love the enthusiasm!" Cree said and followed Primis from the room

Sisue and Gaea walked through the doorway onto the empty planet. The smell in the air was rancid and Gaea crinkled her nose in disgust. In the distance she heard the shriek of the dark energy.

Sisue looked around sadly and said "Even in a world filled with so much life, death leaves it mark."

Gaea nodded "They must be close; the smell is overwhelming."

Sisue waved her hand and the wind carried away the smell from them "Come, would you like to see your father?" Sisue asked

"Yes." Gaea said with a catch in her throat

They walked through the trees until they reached the clearing. Tall hyacinth bushes grew and one towered over the others. Gaea made her way towards it. As she approached the black mist flew up in front of her. A face appeared in the blackness and screamed at her in warning. Sisue held up her hand to it and the golden light drove it back. The black mist stopped shrieking, but held firmly in front of Gaea. Gaea leaned in and studied it closely, without fear.

"What is it?" she asked Sisue in fascination

"It is the dark energy embodied." Sisue told her

"How is this possible? I thought the energies could only ever be harnessed, but did not take form?' Gaea asked

"If a soul resides in it, it may take the form that the soul once possessed." Sisue said sadly

"How is a soul given to the dark energy?" Gaea asked

"Willingly." Sisue said vaguely

Gaea turned to Sisue in confusion "I do not understand."

"It is time for you to know the story of your parents Gaea." Sisue said and the black mist began to shriek again

Sisue held up her left hand and let the golden light reach out to touch it. Once again, the black mist stopped shrieking. Then she held up her right hand and let the silver energy reach out to the black mist. When the three energies touched, they began to swirl around one another slowly. Gaea watched in awe, never had she seen the three energies combined before. It was beautiful to watch as they swirled around in synchronicity.

"Long ago the universe was only one thing Gaea. You know it now as many things, but once it was only a powerful energy combined. Planets and stars did not exist. Beings like ourselves, did not have form, but instead existed in the mass of energy. Life, destruction and love were one thing, the way you see them now. Everything existed in perfect harmony with one another, the infinite." Sisue told her

"What happened to separate them?" Gaea asked in wonderment

"Love." Sisue said "Love became so powerful, that it set the souls free. Love is the only energy that cannot be harnessed or manipulated by anything. Two souls started the universe we know now. Two souls broke the energies apart."

"How?" Gaea asked

"The two souls could no longer exist without form. They longed to feel the touch of the other. To feel the connection, when their souls could touch. To take form, everything had to separate. That is how powerful love can be. It is the most powerful force in the universe and yet it remains elusive. Some even believe it is what formed the energies and the souls. It is believed it was what kept them all connected, until the souls wished for more. It is why we all feel connected to something greater than ourselves. Our souls long to return to the place, where once everything was only one thing." Sisue said

"How terribly sad and terribly beautiful." Gaea said

"It is that longing inside of us that creates music and art. Each soul has its own separate story Gaea. It is love that connects the story of the souls in the most unexplainable ways. Someday the story of your parents will connect to another story in a way we cannot even begin to imagine. That is how powerful love is, it connects us long after our stories have ended." Sisue explained

"How can that be though, when they are both dead?" Gaea asked

"It will connect through you Gaea. The story of Amme and Alyks is about the love that filled their souls. Amme had a choice to make on the day she received her powers. She chose the darkness, so she would have the power to save you. She willingly sacrificed herself, so your story could be told Gaea. Then she willingly gave herself to the darkness to save your father's soul. Inside of that black mist her soul resides, along with your father's." Sisue told her

Gaea gasped at what Sisue was saying "Can't we save them Sisue? There must be a way?" Gaea pleaded

Sisue laughed softly "She does not need saving, Gaea. She is safe in there with him. The dark energy is not something to be feared, do you not see how the golden light and silver energy dance with it right now? They do not fight one another, instead they embrace one another. Each energy holds its own power, but none are meant to be feared. Their souls remain safe in there." Sisue reassured her

"If we are not meant to fear it, then why are the fae always taught to choose the silver string?" Gaea asked "Why are the dark fae shunned like outcasts?"

"Only the strongest fae can wield it Gaea. Fae by their very nature are filled with the kindness of the ethereal energy. Very few understand the power of the dark energy and even fewer still can use it properly. The dark fae can become very dangerous if they are weak and sadly most are." Sisue explained

"Was my mother weak? Is that why it consumed her?" Gaea asked

Sisue looked at Gaea with pride when she spoke of Amme "Your mother is the strongest fae I have ever known. Stronger then even me, the golden light is a rare gift, but not hard to wield. Your mother used the dark energy as it was intended. She saved the only two people she loved with it, that is its power and she understood that."

Gaea finally understood finally, when she was growing up the dark energy was feared by all fae. She had grown up hearing the whispers of the destruction the dark fae had caused. Yet, now as she stood with Sisue, she could see clearly. Only the strongest among them could handle the power of the dark energy

"Reach out now Gaea with your own energy and see for yourself. Close your eyes and meet your parents." Sisue told her

Gaea closed her eyes and let the golden light reach out from her fingertips towards the black mist. The black mist did not fight her, instead it began to envelop the golden light into itself.

When Gaea opened her eyes, she stood in a white room. In front of her stood a man and a woman, holding a baby. The man was tall and had the blackest hair she had ever seen. The woman was only slightly shorter than him and she was gorgeous. The woman laid the baby gently into the cradle and turned back towards Gaea.

"You are as powerful as Sisue said you would be." Amme said to her, absorbing the sight of her and burning it into her memory

"That's funny, Sisue always used to tell me I was powerful like you." Gaea said

"Then you are lucky, indeed. Your mother has a rare strength, embrace it." Alyks told her

Gaea could no longer contain herself. She walked towards them both and let them wrap her in their arms. As the tears streamed down her face, she felt the comfort of their love for the first time ever. She was overwhelmed by it; they had sacrificed so much for her. Now they both held her as if they had never been parted from her.

"I'm so sorry." she sobbed to them both

Alyks took her face in both of his hands "Why are you sorry?" he asked concerned

"For all of the pain I have caused you both." she said

Alyks pulled her tightly to his chest, while Amme stroked

her hair "our poor sweet girl." he soothed "Don't you understand we would have given anything for you?" he asked

"Your father is right Gaea! Tell us you lived a happy life. Tell us you felt safe as a child, because that is all we have ever wanted." Amme told her

"I always felt safe." Gaea told them

"Then our hearts are at peace." Alyks reassured her

When she finally stopped crying, Gaea stepped back to look at them both. Her father stood with his arm around her mother and they both looked so happy. This is the way she always wanted to think of them.

"I am so glad I know how to visit you both! I will come often, I promise." she told them excitedly

Amme's face fell at her words "You cannot come again, Gaea." she said sadly

"What? Why not?' she asked shocked and hurt

Amme held her hand and led her to the window. Outside Gaea could see Sisue held up both hands streaming golden light.

"It is a gift that Sisue gives you now. The dark energy, cannot be held open by you alone. If you tried to come alone, it would consume you Gaea and that is not your fate. Your fate is far greater than us." Amme told her

Gaea looked at her, tears threatening to flow again I can never come back?' she asked heartbroken "I have only just found you and I must say good bye?'

Amme reached out and wiped away the tear that fell down her cheek "We are always with you Gaea. You are the very best parts of us. You are our strength and our courage. Inside of you a piece of both of hearts lives on. You were conceived in the purest form of love we had for one another. Everything you do is a reflection of us."

"You will carry us with you always." Alyks told her

"How can I just leave, knowing you are both trapped in here." Gaea asked desperately

"We are not trapped; we are at peace here. Our souls will never be separated again. Someday, you may know a love like ours and then you will understand." Amme said and let go of her hand to take Alyks's

"What if I don't though? How will I ever understand what the two of you gave up for me?' she asked

"We can't know our own fate, Gaea. Our souls will tell the story that is hidden deep inside of them. To know where our story ends would be useless, without the experience of it all. Your story has only just begun, but it will be filled with pain and sadness. It will also be filled with joy and unexpected happiness. Stop worrying about how it ends and focus on the telling of it. Be so amazing that your name will never be forgotten." Alyks counseled

Outside they all heard Sisue call her name and Gaea said "I must go."

They both hugged her quickly and said their goodbyes "We love you." Amme whispered to her right before she closed her eyes

Gaea opened her eyes and turned around, lowering her hand. Sisue slowly, let the golden light fade and the black mist began to disappear.

"So, they are gone from me forever now?" Gaea asked sadly

"Only if you forget their words Gaea. Besides, no one is ever truly gone from us." she reminded her "Come, we have work to do."

Gaea followed her until they reached the rotting corpses. Gaea bent down and began to scrape samples from them into tubes. This was the only DNA that still existed of the humans. Gaea had been chosen to help start a new experiment on earth with a team of scientists. It was to be led by the Lagorian named Primis, but they had all been advised to keep a close eye on him. She hoped the humans would be successful this time. She was sure under the proper supervision of the group; the experiment would be a success.

CHAPTER 20

Caspian and Cree stood on a hillside and looked down at the first humans on earth. They were a crude looking bunch and had chosen to use the caves as their shelter.

"What is that strange emotion you are feeling?' Cree asked Caspian about the emotion running through him as he watched the humans

"It is called hope." Caspian answered

"It is very odd and it feels weak compared to your other emotions. What is it used to express?" Cree asked

"Hope is like a small glimmer of light in a dark room. It means that a small part of me can see something good may come of this." Caspian explained

"Why?" Cree asked curiously

Caspian shrugged unable to explain further "I'm not sure."

"Well, that seems very stupid." Cree scoffed "You know exactly what happened on Huma. Given the facts, I would think hope is the last emotion you would have."

"Perhaps, but that is the beauty of hope, Cree. It doesn't have to make sense to be felt." Caspian replied

Below them one of the men picked up a rock and hit the other one over the head with it. He took the food the man had and sat down beside him and began eating it.

Cree clapped his hands gleefully at the sight of it "Well

done cave man!" he hollered down at him

The frightened man looked up and saw the Twins standing on the hill and began running in terror away from them.

"Now you have exposed yourself to the human." Caspian chastised "He might think we are deities or something. What if they have to start the experiment all over again?"

"He is eating raw meat Caspian, if that doesn't kill something else soon will! Besides they do not even have language yet, who is he going to tell?" Cree laughed and rolled his eyes

The frightened man ran straight to the safety of his cave. He grabbed a sharp rock and began to scratch into the wall of his cave. He carved the image of the two men he had just seen. It came out crudely, like a child's drawing, but the two stick figures came out looking identical.

Danby opened his eyes slowly and sat up. He could not remember how he had gotten here. All he could remember was the witch reaching into Ian's chest and killing him. He looked around and could see he was very high up, wherever he was.

Then he noticed the strange man, with the milky white skin. The hairless man sat staring at him, wearing a robe.

"Who are you?' Danby asked

"I am Primis." the being said

"Have you finally come to save us?" Danby asked, unsure if he was already dead

"I have come to help you save yourself." Primis said and stood up

Danby stood up, although his legs felt very shaky. He

walked a few steps and immediately recognized where they were. He was on top of the tower of the witch queen.

"Where am I?" he asked suspiciously

"Huma has been destroyed. I am afraid you are the last pure human alive." Primis informed him

"Did the witch destroy it?" Danby asked angrily

"If you are referring to Queen Amme of Thelry, then yes." Primis replied

"Then I will kill her." Danby hissed

"Queen Amme has been dead for centuries; she was destroyed with Huma." Primis informed him

"Centuries?" Danby said confused

"To you it feels as if it just happened, but it was centuries ago. Cree kept you in stasis, until I could return here to help you." Primis said

"Help me with what?" Danby asked

"You are going to rebuild the human race, Danby. You are the only pure blood left from the original humans. Your DNA will build the future here. Cree has obtained two hundred of the finest Thelrians to serve you. We will build a lab and soon enough we will have more humans. In the meantime, these people will serve you and their offspring will serve all of the human generations to come." Primis told him

"You are staying then?' Danby asked hopefully

"For a while, but I have other duties. A team is trying to resurrect the species on earth also, but their samples are corrupted with magic. This planet will be left under your rule, Cree has assured me, you will keep the human bloodline clean. We cannot rebuild the race if the DNA is corrupted." Primis told him

"I will not fail you." Danby said

"Good then let us go and mee the people you now rule over. We have much to accomplish." Primis told him

"Is this the planet Fae?" Danby asked'

"It is, but Cree has gifted it to us, so you may name it anything you wish." Primis told him

"What was the name of the first city on Huma?" Danby asked having a hard time recalling the history of first man

"The first humans named it hell." Primis said recalling it fondly

"Then I declare this to be Hell." Danby said enacting his first law

In the distance the black mist saw the face of the human and it began shrieking.

Dear Readers,
I hope you are enjoying the way the storyline is heading. I wanted to go back and see what led to Sawyer's creation. Next up I will be writing the history of Mother. I always thought Mother

deserved her own storyline, because she had so much life before Sawyer. Enjoy!
Shawna Bennett

www.ingramcontent.com/pod-product-compliance
Lightning Source LLC
Chambersburg PA
CBHW061532120726

48001CB00004B/1509